Budleigh and Rexford

by

Sarah Powell and Tony Hazel

Two Kittens Publishing
The Whitehouse, West Street, Sompting BN15 0AP
info@two-kittens-publishing.co.uk

Hardback Edition 2019
ISBN 978-1-9997079-5-8

Budleigh and Rexford
by
Sarah Powell and Tony Hazel

with

Illustrations by Tony Hazel

Chapter 1

Budleigh looked at his breakfast, plump pretty peach pieces on silver grape leaves. He cracked a half-cracked laugh. "Pitches, plump-a pitches!"

This had been Budleigh's only meal for six weeks straight and it was taking its toll. "Pitches, plump-a pitches," he gently sobbed; small strings of spittle elasticating at the corners of sore lips. "Plump-a," he sniffed. He was sore from ear'oles to breakfast time.

Intermittently, when he became bound solid by the unvarying goose egg diet that his captors insisted was good for him, plump peaches were peeled. These would then be administered, with the greatest kindness, until such time as the dam burst and Budleigh became a hollow tube. On days like these, you could have played him like a rusty tin whistle.

Budleigh's tired eyes focused vacantly on the blue outside the window: he ached to feel the sun on his face, the wind in his hair. Four tapped lightly on the door. "What is it-a?" roared Budleigh, with as much roar as he could muster from his sore, cracked lips. Four entered tentatively, carrying a silver tray of brushes, a long black comb and a mirror. "I thought I-I may re-plait your beard today sir," he stammered. Budleigh's eyes rolled back in his head. "Get out-a! How-a many times-a do I have-a to tell you-a??" He sunk back in the chair. Four left the tray on the polished oak dresser, hopeful that, one day, Budleigh would take an interest. Being hairdresser to Budleigh Salterton was not the easiest job!

At length, Budleigh hauled himself from the chair and walked towards the tray. He plucked the silver-backed mirror from it, noticing the deeply veined skin on his hands, and held it up to his face. He looked at the cracks round his lips, the pomegranate purple tinge of his skin, the wrinkled lines of despair imprinted on his forehead and the hollow staring eyes. Night after night, he dreamed of putting these veiny hands round a pompous rat's neck or a spiteful little girl's. He wasn't fussy which.

In an adjacent room, Rexford Overstreet was pirouetting in front of a full length mirror. Ten, Three and Six were in attendance, holding the train of a cascading silken dress, fold after fold of damask lace tumbling to the floor over golden, square-toed shoes. Rexford smiled contentedly. Of course he would have preferred embroidered pantaloons but, in their absence, he was prepared to settle for the finest finery the castle had on offer, even if it was a dress.

....

In the early days of their incarceration, Rexford had spent a lot of time angrily pacing about the castle. He and Budleigh had done their best to avoid each other, as there was a lot of bad blood between them. They had tried to continue fighting but, whenever they'd headed towards each other, the footmen appeared and separated them. So, after a week or two of frustrating non-fighting, they had given up and retreated into their own worlds. Budleigh had closeted himself in his room to fume.

Rexford, on the other hand, had begun to roam the castle. He'd spent his days examining every nook and cranny. He hadn't known what he was looking for, but it had made him feel better to be doing something.

....

One day, as he marched up an endless staircase, he had found himself in a turret he hadn't noticed before. Pushing open the door, he'd looked around and seen a large pink slipper shaped bath. Walking up to it, he saw it was lightly padded.

"Hmmm," he thought. "A padded bath, eh?"

Looking around further, he then noticed a hundred feather mattresses with a hundred silken sheets neatly folded by their side.

"How did I miss that?!" he mused.

To be fair, each mattress was quite thin and they all sat in quite a deep mattress shaped hole, so only the top ten protruded. He edged up to the bed and gently sat on it. He shifted a little further back and gave it a little bounce. "Mmm, comfy," he thought.

Getting up, Rexford wandered toward a large heavily carved wardrobe. Reaching for the handles, he hesitated, suddenly feeling as if he were being watched. Shaking his head, he grasped the handles and wrenched the doors open. The sight that greeted him made him squeal with delight. He clapped a paw over his snout, feeling a bit silly, but then again.....

Rexford, being the son of a successful businessman, had rarely wanted for anything. He had been brought up with the finest of the fine. Cars, art, food, no expense had been spared. Above all these things, with the exception of food, (he was a rat after all) his first love was clothes. While he had been dressed in his finery when he arrived at the castle, that had been quite a while ago and he was starting to smell. The pristine dresses before him represented cleanliness and elegance. Without hesitation, he grabbed the nearest, prettiest frock he could see. Tearing off his filthy clothes, he stood there naked, grappling with a dainty zip. Finally releasing it, he thrust a chubby leg into the opening. Hopping like a demented mannequin, he twirled backwards in the voluminous dress, tripping and falling into the empty bath, legs flailing, material shredding. It was then that the door swung open and Three and Nine were greeted with a sight that no being should have to witness.

"Sir!" they gasped in unison. "What on earth....?"

They didn't get a chance to finish the sentence: Rexford's head surfaced somewhere between the torn fabric and half a hairy leg.

"I, I can explain..."

The footmen gave each other a look, then a smile. "No need to explain sir: we understand." They moved toward him and gently helped him out of the bath and out of the dress. Nine had retrieved one of Porcelaina's bathrobes; he held it open patiently, while Rexford struggled into the oversized pink sleeves.

"Leave it to us, sir. We'll attend to this."

Three began to run the bath. "Just like the old days," he whispered to Nine. They both smiled. "I'll light the candles."

....

Cord softly calls his Boggis.

Amelia delicately steps through clear tessellations of light and stands at Bangle's side. She will always be The Cat: she is enjoying her femininity, her cattiness and her dimensions. She has absorbed every aspect of Amelia; she loves Pearl as fiercely and loyally as Amelia had done before her.

Cord smiles warmly at the Boggis, knowing its every thought. Cracking the knuckles of both hands, he extends a white arm, The Cat jumps nimbly onto his gloved hand.

"Do you remember," Cord asks, "clanging around in that suit of armour, being beaten into a pile of bones by a little girl called Porcelaina?" He already knows the answer, and so does the Boggis, so no more needs to be said.

"I know how happy you are in your new body," Cord continues; he knows it's more than just a body now, it's a mind and personality. "I've watched you grow into yourself, and I want you to know how proud I am!" The Boggis arches and purrs, in spite of itself, flattery, after years of flatness, is addictive.

"Well, of course, you will always be Amelia, but I will need a little help from your extra Boggis power. We have some training to do." He waves his other arm to reveal a sea of maps, storyboards, tubes and pipes, images of people: matchstick people, hieroglyphic people, flat like playing cards, stacked, not one on top of another, but intermingled, only with more tubes, veins and pulsating arteries.

The Cat immediately recognises the moving drawings: an army of baby Boggis.

Chapter 2

Budleigh had, for some time, been formulating an escape plan. Despite his fondness for the warm milk and bedtime biscuit, lovingly proffered by Ten every night, he had noticed that he never remembered getting into bed once he had finished it. So instead of drinking it, in the last few days, he had been taking a mouthful without swallowing. Unfolding the napkin, dabbing at his mouth and then.... waking in the morning, in bed as usual. Undaunted, he persevered. It must have been a week of drinking the milk, not drinking the milk, eating the biscuit without the milk, with the milk, blowing his nose on the napkin, taking the napkin and waving it above his head, all with the same result: he would find himself in bed in the morning with no recollection of how he got there. Then it dawned on him, it was the napkin. The napkin was drugged! That night he ate the biscuit, drank the milk and with his gloved hand, carefully unfolded the napkin and placed it back on the tray. Closing both eyes, he pretended to fall into a deep sleep.

In the dead of night, Budleigh flicked open one eye and then the other, looked around and rose from his bed. He quickly slipped out of the night dress, the footmen insisted he wear, and into his own clothes. At first, he had refused to wear the nightdress, but the footmen had nagged him so politely and so relentlessly, keeping him awake for a week, that he had caved in to their demand. They had allowed him to choose which one to wear, so he chose the one with the least frou-frou and frills and picked off the bows whenever he could. Six sewed them back on every time.

Dressed in black, Budleigh blended into the night. He moved silently to the door. Opening it just a crack, he blinked into the gloom. It took a while before his eyes adjusted to the darkness. Looking around, he saw the landing was empty. Footmen would usually patrol the castle at night, sweeping with their twiggy brooms, dusting and straightening pictures. Tonight, they were absent. Budleigh slowly opened the door, careful not to let it creak. Climbing down the stairs, he made for the corridor below. Despite being a prisoner in the castle for some time, he had never been out of his room on his own. He felt unexpectedly nervous. The awful routine the footmen subjected him to had made him lose something of his old self. For the first time in a long time, Budleigh felt anxious. Pausing at the top of the stairs, he felt his chest tighten and a lump grow in his throat. He suddenly felt the urge to turn and head back up the stairs to his room. "Get-a grip-a," Budleigh whispered to himself. He swallowed hard and tiptoed down the stairs. When he rounded the corner, the sight he encountered made him stop dead in his tracks. There in front of him stood the twelve footmen. They had arranged themselves in a semicircle, each one facing the back of the one in front. In each left hand they held a large brass key and they were softly chanting...

"Wind up. Wind up. Yes sir, yes sir. Wind up me, I wind up you...."

With this, they each took their key and lifted the jacket of the man in front.

"Wind up, wind up. This is for you sir. This is for me."

They each placed the key into a socket under the fabric waistcoat of the man in front and with a click, they all stopped. Budleigh stood, open mouthed, watching the scene unfold before him. The footmen were clockwork!

Then One, with a shrill cry, grabbed the key in the back of Two and, with both hands, gave it a sharp turn to the left. Two then did the same with the key of Three and so on, until each footmen had received one full turn. There followed a brief pause and then a frenzy of shrieking and winding which made Budleigh feel very uncomfortable and a little scared: so much so, that a small yelp unexpectedly shot from his mouth. At once, the footmen stopped and turned toward the direction of the noise. Budleigh clapped a hand to his mouth and rapidly considered his options. The footmen, who were shocking jailers, always fussing and nagging, were now a sinister group of clockwork men! Thinking fast, Budleigh decided that it would probably be better if he wasn't there and headed for Rexford's room. He took the stairs, two at time, and burst in. "Rex-a. Rex-a. Wake up-a!"

Rexford was snuggled down in his bed. His face, covered in night cream and he had large curlers in, although his fur wasn't quite long enough to go all the way around them. He was cuddling a small teddy bear and sucking his thumb.

"Rex-a. Wake up-a!" Budleigh grabbed Rexford and shook him violently.   Rexford snuffled. Budleigh really shook him this time. "REX-A!"

Overstreet woke with a start. "What?!" he blinked against the light, dropping his teddy in the process.

"It's the footmen. They're-a clock-a-work!"

"So?" said Rexford, turning over to go back to sleep.

"This-a changes everything. We might-a be able to-a dismantle them, make a contraption and make our escape-a!"

"Escape?" said Rexford. "Why would we want to escape? We have everything we need here...."

With this, Budleigh grabbed the recumbent rat and lifted him out of bed. He looked him squarely in the eye. He was shaking with rage.

"Why didn't you say you wanted to leave? Why, we can leave whenever we like!"

"What-a? How-a?" Budleigh dropped Rexford.

Rexford recovered the fallen bear and swept its ears back, straightening its tiny bow tie.

"Dear boy. Sit down and listen."

Chapter 3

"This-a had better be good-a!" growled Budleigh as Rexford gathered himself and prepared to spin the tale of their imprisonment.

"The trouble with you Salterton, is that you take everything so literally. No imagination."

Budleigh clenched a fist. Overstreet was starting to push his luck.

"Where are we?" asked Overstreet.

Budleigh thought for a moment, then realised he didn't know. Budleigh was generally much brighter than Rexford, but his sort of cleverness came from a straightforward approach to life. If he met a problem, he would tackle it head on, using intellectual brute force to smash it to pieces. Rexford, on the other hand, whilst not so clever, had a much more devious nature, as befitting a rat.

"I don't know-a," Budleigh sighed.

"Well I do, or rather I don't, but I know someone who does."

"Well-a, what are you waiting for-a? Get us out of here-a!"

"All in good time dear boy. All in good time. As a

precaution, I had a homing device implanted in my ear. See?" he pointed to a small bulge in his right ear. "What with all the trouble with that pompous idiot Horattus, I didn't want to take the chance that he would have me kidnapped and no one would know where I was, so I had this homing beacon implanted in my ear, so I could always be found. It's just a matter of time until we're rescued. All I have to do is activate it..."

It was at this point that Budleigh snapped. "What-a! You mean you haven't-a turned it on-a!?"

"I was enjoying the rest. It's been like staying in the finest hotel. Every need catered for, and no bill at the end of it!"

Budleigh launched himself across the room. With a single bound had Rexford tightly round the throat and was shaking him for all he was worth.

"Turn it on-a! Turn it on-a!"
Budleigh shook him again.

"Turn it on-a! Turn it on-a!"

Rexford started to turn blue. His eyes, rolling back in his head.

"Gurk... wheeze... OK. OK... just stop squeezing.. gak!"

Abruptly, Budleigh dropped the limp rodent, who fell into a gasping crumpled heap on the floor.

After a few seconds, Rexford regained his composure. He reached up with his left hand, felt for the lump in his right ear and gave it a gentle squeeze. A dim red light flickered into life and began to slowly pulse in the half light of Rexford's bedroom. "Now we wait," Rexford coughed hoarsely.

Budleigh, still snarling, stood back, sat on Rexford's bed, folded his arms and waited.

....

In his haste, Budleigh had forgotten the footmen. Their pursuit had been painfully slow as, of course, they couldn't move until they had all been fully wound, which was a complex and time-consuming business.

"Idiots!" muttered Budleigh. "They're not-a going to be taking over the world-a any time soon-a!"

Before the words had left his lips, they heard the clanking of twelve clockwork men, heading up the stone stairs decisively towards Rexford's bedroom. Budleigh had just enough time to take three giant steps across the room, slam the heavy oak door shut and lock it before the footmen clamoured for admittance.

"Thank god for Rexford's vanity!" thought Budleigh. The footmen had allowed him the privilege of a key to 'protect my modesty while I'm changing'. Budleigh wasn't stupid enough to think the footmen wouldn't have a master key, but it would take them a while to fetch it. Searching hurriedly round the room, he rammed a heavy table and chairs in front of the door for good measure.

Chapter 4

On a control panel in Rexfords HQ, a small red light flickered into life and emitted a slow yet steady ping.

Some time later, Sniffer McGurk entered the control room.

Since Rexford had gone, life had got a little lax around Lower Rattopia. Most of the things that Rexford liked doing, such as riding around and shouting, bullying and generally being horrid, had slipped by the wayside. His gang - Sniffer McGurk, Three Fingers Smith and Cringer Wilson - had quickly returned to Lower Rattopia once both Budleigh and Rexford had been imprisoned. Despite their attempted treachery, Budleigh had proved no better a boss than Rexford, and although they could have gone anywhere, they missed Rexford because, despite all his shortcomings, he had at least remembered their birthdays, and no one else had done that, not even their own mothers! So they waited for Rexford to return.

Sniffer didn't notice the light at first. He was walking down a corridor on his way to the kitchen to make a snack, as it was almost half an hour until tea time and he was hungry, when he heard a ping coming from what he thought was a cupboard. He pushed the door open with one finger and peered into the gloom. A red glow ebbed and flowed in the darkness. He fumbled for the switch and flicked the light on. It was Rexford's control room. He had never been in here before. Rexford wouldn't allow anyone in, as it was here he monitored and controlled the goings on in Lower Rattopia. Looking around the room, Sniffer could see banks of monitors, switches, computers. To his left, was a big red button with the word 'ON' underneath it. Without a second thought, he pushed it; the control room sprang into life. Light twinkled and screens faded into view. Looking closely at the monitors, he could see all parts of Lower Rattopia - market square, tavern, post office, council offices and the army's barracks. Concealed cameras focused electronic eyes on everyone and everywhere. Control panels, covered in switches, dials and knobs too numerous to count, chattered away together, an AI city. Amongst the cacophony of technology, was what looked like a radar screen, green, with a sweeping light rotating about a central axis, emitting a solitary ping, and a soft amber light at about 90 degrees to the perpendicular.

Chapter 5

Rexford struggled to his feet and looked at the barricaded door. The footmen couldn't get their key into the lock, as Budleigh had left his jammed in. Being only slight in stature, their attempts to charge it made little impact on the heavy door, as they ineffectively tried to break it down with a series of insubstantial shoulder barges.

"So if you have a plan-a, now would be a good-a time to activate it-a!" Budleigh snarled at Rexford.

"Patience, patience," retorted Rexford. After ten or so minutes of banging, silence descended. From without, came the sound of muffled discussion. The two inmates strained to hear the conversation, but it was just too far away and too quiet for them to discern any of its contents. This continued for another couple of minutes, until silence reigned once more.

"Do you think-a they've gone-a?" Budleigh whispered.

"I hope not," Rexford hissed back, his ear still flashing.

Apparently from nowhere, a great whiteness descends on them. A whiteness so white that neither of them can tell up from down, left from right or back from front. The all enveloping whiteness leaves them dizzy and unsteady on their feet. From the whiteness, steps an elegant figure, totally dressed in white, so as to make it appear he is but a head and a smile.

"Now now gentlemen. What have we here?" says Cord Bangle, for it is he.

Budleigh makes to lurch at Cord, in an attempt to grab him, but Cord is too quick and freezes Budleigh in mid leap.

"Hello Bangle."

"Ah, Overstreet. Rexford Overstreet. I was coming to see you anyway, the footmen merely hastened my visit." He reaches out a hand and plucks the homing device from Rexford's ear, much as a magician might produce an egg from the ear of a volunteer. He holds the device between thumb and forefinger, inspecting its bleeping redness, which, against the impenetrable whiteness, plunges the space into a sparking scintillating strawberry shake. He wafts his other hand across it and extinguishes the light.

....

Sniffer stared at the screen. As suddenly as it had started, the pinging stopped and the amber light went out. "Oh," he cried, spinning this way and that. "Who's there?" He was answered only by the growl from his stomach, reminding him his snack was long overdue.

....

"This will never do, Rexford. You know why you're here?"

Even though Rexford isn't entirely sure, he feels it is best to play along with the dimension-hopping entity for the time being at least.

"Yes?" he answers none too convincingly. "I did a bad thing?"

"You did Rexford, you did. Kidnapping, unlawful incarceration, assault and battery, theft and treason. You're a double crossing, lying, cheating bully who would sell his own grandmother for a bacon sandwich. To put not too fine a point on it, Rexford Overstreet, you are bad from the soles of your paws to the tips of your whiskers."

Rexford looks at the ground, twirling the bow on his tailor-made nightie."

"Well, what have you to say for yourself?"

"Sorry," mutters Rexford.

"Pardon? I didn't quite hear that."

"Sorry."

"Come again?"

"Sorry!"

"That's more like it. Now will you be doing it again?"

"No."

Cord cocks an eyebrow.

"No I won't."

"Promise?"

"I promise."

"Very well, then you may leave."

"Great!" exclaims a relieved rat, Budleigh will be pleased.

"In a year."

"A year!?!"

"Yes, a year," and with that, he releases Budleigh, who promptly falls to the ground. He hauls himself up and shakes his head.

"Ah my head-a," he feels under his top hat for lumps.

With a sweep of his arm, Cord removes the barricades and a key turns in the lock. The whiteness starts to dissolve; footmen flood into the room, Four clutching an extra large hair brush, just in case. As Cord turns to leave, Rexford sees his chance. Cord opens a door into the brightness and exits through it: as it is just about to close, Rexford grabs his teddy bear and throws it into the crack, wedging it open.

Seizing his chance, Rexford dives for the chink and squeezes through. He was enjoying his holiday, but even Rexford isn't so work-shy he can continue it for another year. Budleigh, who is still a little dazed, takes a moment longer, but he too manages to shimmy his way past the door, which slams shut with a terminal clunk. They have both escaped their prison, but to where exactly?

Chapter 6

Budleigh and Rexford looked at each other and then around at what surrounds them - an inky blackness enveloping them every bit as much as the whiteness had done just a few seconds ago. Cord was nowhere to be seen and neither was the ground. They both looked at their feet. Nope, no ground.

"Are we falling?" asked Rexford.

"I'm-a not entirely sure-a," replied Budleigh.

The blackness was so black, the only reference point each of them had, was each other. Gradually, a gentle whooshing began in their ears. Rexford's fur began to stir and Budleigh placed a hand on his top hat to steady it in the increasing breeze.

The initial whoosh now became a gale that grew louder and louder. Rexford struggled to keep his nightgown from blowing off over his head and Budleigh grasped the brim of his hat with both hands.

"Are we going to die?" screamed Rexford into the hurricane that blew from beneath them.

"Maybe-a," mouthed Budleigh back at him, his words lost in the howling wind.

Very gradually, Budleigh and Rexford began to drift apart.

Rexford reached out for Budleigh and Budleigh reached for Rexford. They really didn't like each other, but in this strange other world, each was all the other had. In the nick of time, their fingertips met and Budleigh grasped Rexford's wrist.

They were definitely falling, only it wasn't down. They were falling up. They could tell this now, as a tiny pinpoint of purple light appeared above their heads. Larger and larger it grew, until it became inevitable they were going to slam into it at a terrific speed.

"Is this it? Is this how it all ends, pulverised into purple puree?" mourned Rexford.

Closer and closer they rushed toward the pulsating purple patch.

"Good-a-bye cruel-a world-a," burbled a broken Budleigh.

They closed their eyes and braced themselves for impact.

A few seconds later, Rexford gingerly peeked through his mostly closed eyes. Were they dead? He could still feel Budleigh's hand tightly gripping his wrist. He fully flicked an eye open and took a look at Budleigh. He was crouched in the brace position, ready for impact. Both eyes still tightly shut, his knuckles white and welded to Rexford's arm, he opened the other eye and stood up.

"Would you mind letting go, old man? My paw has gone numb."

Still crouching, Budleigh opened one eye and saw Rexford standing before him. Realising he still had Rexford's wrist tightly grasped, he quickly let go, as if his arm were something unpleasant that had crept up his sleeve uninvited.

He opened the other eye and drew himself up to his full height. Rexford looked at Budleigh, Budleigh looked at Rexford, each not daring to look around them.

Breaking their gaze, they both turned toward the enormous palm tree standing before them in bright purple sand. The tree was so big, that when they lifted their heads and tracked up the mighty trunk, they both toppled backwards. It's just as well they did, for at that precise moment, a gigantic orange coconut hurtled toward them from the top of the tree.

"Run-a!" shouted Budleigh. They staggered to their feet. With millimeters to spare, the colossal coconut crashed to the sand with a deafening thump. The two escapees fell to the ground again and sat in silence, regarding the huge orange orb.

"Where are we?" asked Rexford.

"I have-a no idea-a. I'm not-a sure I like it, wherever we are-a."

Looking past the giant nut, they saw bright purple sand. It was a very intense colour and full of what looked like shells, only they weren't like any shells they'd ever seen before. Most normal shells have an animal inside them, the shell protecting its occupant. These shells looked odd. What was it? Neither could be sure, everything looked like it should do, but didn't do.

Budleigh picked one out of the sand and took a closer look.

As he did so, the shell let out a piercing scream. Budleigh was so astonished by the loudness of the squeal, he dropped it immediately. The dissonant din rose, as every shell on the beach yelled at Budleigh and Rex. They clamped their hands over their ears. After a shrill minute, that seemed to go on a good deal longer than sixty seconds, the noise died away. Bending down, Rexford looked closely at the shells. Each shell was, in fact, a small animal. The animals, at least that's what Rexford assumed them to be, had six legs and were clutching a tiny dollop of goo to each of their tiny chests. The goo was also purple, but a slightly different shade to that of the sand, more amethyst. Budleigh bent down and peered at the creatures.

"What are they Rex-a?"

"I'm not sure, but don't touch them again!"

The odd creatures seemed to be holding the goo very tightly. They looked even more closely at the shells. Abruptly, the creature they were examining, took the tiny glob and produced a tiny sling. With great force, it hurled the amethyst glob directly toward Rexford, hitting him squarely between the eyes. The ghastly gobbit was still attached to the creature as it started to run round and round Rexford.

"What on earth is going on?" shouted Rexford. The creature picked up speed.

Suddenly, another glob was fired, at Budleigh this time, hitting him in the midriff. The lobber enthusiastically encircled him, followed by another creature and another globule, then another and another.

"I don't like-a the way this is going-a!" shouted Budleigh, starting to run, but there was now so much muck covering him that his feet and arms became tangled in the sticky substance. Rexford too, was being trussed up by the industrious urchins. Before their brains had a chance to catch up with the lightning fast rotations, they were tied, very tightly, together.

"What is happening?" shouted Rexford, as the little creatures began to drag the pair of fugitives to the ground. Soon, the tipping point was reached, Rexford and Budleigh toppled into the sand. Budleigh landed on top of a face-planted Rexford, who was struggling to get the purple powder out of his nose and mouth; it had stuck to the remains of his face cream, making him look like a half finished finger painting by a five year old. After a short pause, they felt a tugging at their bonds, as they were slowly rolled onto their sides.

"Thspa," spluttered Rexford, ejecting the odious grit. They rested on the sand for a second, before Budleigh began to struggle, but he was bound so tightly he could barely breathe, let alone consider an escape. After a few more seconds, they felt another tug on the gelatinous gloop, and were neatly packaged in a purple pupae. The tugging became more determined, as the shell creatures, chattering like chipmunks, surely but slowly dragged Budleigh and Rexford from the beach into the bright blue bushes.

Chapter 7

"Rex-a, Rex-a, can you speak-a?"
"Just about," spluttered Rexford. "What is this place?"

The land the two jailbirds had fallen into, was quite unlike anything either of them had ever seen before. The creatures diligently dragged the bound pair through thick jungle. Inching along, they started to notice their environment, which prompted a variety of emotions. Rexford was fascinated by the colours. Eyes wide open, he stared in wonder at the strange kaleidoscopic swirls whirling about him. Budleigh, appalled and nauseous, was more in touch with his self-preservation instinct than his aesthetic appreciation. Most of the plants were orange and an odd shade of blue. The violet sky held a tiny blue sun, which whilst small, was very hot. Deeper and deeper into jungle, the shell creatures dragged them, their maniacal laughter ringing through the blue branches. Onwards they pulled, tugging and hauling in a surprisingly synchronised rhythm.

"Where do you think they're taking us?"
"I think-a we're going to find out-a soon enough-a."

After some time, neither of them could be sure how long, the tiny creatures stopped. One by one, they began the process of disentangling themselves from the hapless duo. Each sticky string was carefully detached, coiled up and returned to its owner's sling. Once the last of the bonds were finally removed, the pair struggled to a seated position.

"What now-a?" Budleigh began, but before Rexford could answer, a very large hand swept down from the sky and scooped them up. This was a very unusual day!

"Well, well, what have we here?" boomed the owner of the hand. Budleigh and Rexford let out a strangled, but unified cry of alarm.

"Gerk!"

"Gerk to you, my little strangers. Welcome to Purpolia. My name is Garvandulan Spang. And who might you be?"

Rexford tried to speak, but having snapped out of his psychedelic daydream, he found his mouth bone dry and unable to help him. Budleigh rose to his feet, adjusted his attire and straightened his hat, which, amazingly, had stayed adhered to his head throughout the journey.

"My name-a is Budleigh. Budleigh Salterton. But you can call me Mr Salterton!" he proclaimed as he stamped his big black boot into Garvandulan's palm.

"Budleigh Salterton. What an unusual name!" said Garvandulan. "And what about your pet, does it have a name?" Rexford suddenly rediscovered the power of speech.

"Pet! Pet! I, sir, am no one's pet. Pet indeed! I've had men broken for less impudence than that! I sir, am Rexford Overstreet, Lord of Lower Rattopia and heir to the Overstreet fortune! I am a very important rat!" He, too, then stamped his paw into Garvandulan's palm and adjusted his nightgown, inflating his chest like a puffer fish meeting a shark.

Garvandulan Spang smiled wryly and gently closed his palm. Depositing the two tearaways into his waistcoat pocket, he set off for the Purpopolis.

Chapter 8

The giant's pocket was cosy, dark and warm. After such a long and arduous journey, Budleigh and Rexford almost immediately fell into a deep sleep.

Sometime later, Budleigh was the first to wake. He blinked against the darkness. Shaking his head, he rubbed his eyes and squinted once more into the gloom. Tottering to his feet, he tripped in the fabric gully he found himself traversing. Opposite, he could just make out a round, recumbent rat, softly snoring and snuffling, still wearing his nightie and gently sucking his thumb. Budleigh's eyes strained into the murk. His senses went through the gears. Sight? Not great. Sound? Muted, apart from Rex snoring. Taste? N/A. Touch? He feels the walls. The walls didn't feel very wall-y, more knitware-y. He groped through the dark and examined the surface of the wall more carefully, 'Ah, cable-a stitch-a,' he thought to himself.

Before he could do another thing, Budleigh was gently picked from the pocket by Garvandulan and very carefully set down on a huge wooden table in a very large room.

"Gerk to you Mr Salterton," Garvandulan Spang politely announced. He was speaking in a very quiet voice, so as not to wake Rexford.

"What-a are you on about-a?" bellowed an inconsiderate Budleigh, "I'm-a starving, got any ham-a sandwiches, giant?"

Garvandulan looked down on Budleigh and plucked him from the table by the scruff of his neck. With Budleigh pinched between his thumb and forefinger, he walked over to a large dresser on the wall opposite, its shelves choked with displays of dinner plates and special pieces of unnecessary crockery. Among them was a large glass jar. The jar was used to hold freshly cut flowers, flowers which always seemed to fill the kitchen. Spang took the jar down and attempted to place Budleigh inside it.

However, Budleigh was having none of this and kicked and swung wildly against his captor. As he was lowered into the jar, he made like a starfish in the top, in an attempt to prevent his insertion.

Budleigh managed to brace himself across the narrow neck, however Garvandulan was equally determined to ensure Budleigh's incapacity and while using one hand to press Salterton toward the bottom of the jar, he began to flick at Budleigh's arms and legs from the rim of the jar. As soon as he would flick at an arm or leg, momentarily dislodging it, the loose limb would immediately shoot back out again and re-adhere itself to the rim: and so this continued for several minutes, getting faster and faster. "What-a are you doing-a you maniac-a?" Budleigh shouted as Garvandulan flicked.

Garvandulan decided to change tactics and lifted Budleigh away from the mouth of the jar. Wrapping his large hands around Budleigh, he posted him though the top of the jar. He was almost completely inside when he managed to shoot his legs out and catch the rim of the jar with his feet.

"Get in there..." said a mildly irked Spang; he wiped his feet from the rim of the jar and Budleigh plummeted in at high speed. He landed on his head. Fortunately, he was wearing his top hat and it broke his fall, leaving him shaken not blurred. The hat itself fared quite badly, being concertinaed by Budleigh's pile driven landing. Righting himself, he picked up the flattened hat, angrily punching the crumpled topper into a vague top hat shape and then resolutely returning the battered sausage to his head.

Readjusting his senses, he looked at the walls of the jar and up to its entrance, assessing his chance of an exit. It wasn't looking good. The walls of the jar were smooth and sheer, curving away from him into the sunlight. The entrance/exit wasn't too far above his head, but there was nowhere he could get any purchase to begin the climb.

"Why-a have you put-a me in here-a? Budleigh shouted at Spang.

Garvandulan looked in the jar and chuckled "This is where I'd like you to stay, while I make you some lunch my little friend. You don't want the cat to get you, do you?"

The Cat? Salterton slightly winced at the memory of the little grey cat he'd shot in Rexford's dungeon. He also considered how large cats might be here - probably bigger than tigers! Budleigh did not want to see any cats at all, let alone cats that might be bigger than a bus!

Budleigh looked around and saw Spang making ham sandwiches in the middle distance. Salterton scanned the room. Yes, this was definitely a kitchen. There was a large stove in the middle of one wall; a sink and larder filled another wall. Budleigh continued to look around through the wobbly glass. In the far corner he saw a door, slightly ajar.

From behind, Budleigh heard a four-footed *phlump*. He froze. In the next instant, he spun around to find a huge pair of emerald eyes staring at him. Stepping back, he saw massive twiggy whiskers and a snuffling, forensic nose pressed firmly against the glass.

It was a cat!

No, not just any cat.

THE CAT!

And it was huge. And it really wasn't looking at all happy!

Chapter 9

"Hello Budleigh," said the Grey Cat.

"GERK!!!" yelled Budleigh. "What-a are you doing here-a!?"

"I might ask you the same thing!" spat back the Cat.

"B-b-but-a I killed you-a! I shot you dead-a!"

"You did indeed. Clean through the heart. Dead as you like," said the Cat.

Budleigh was very confused. He shot the Cat, it's what brought Porcelaina's parents out from hiding. He could still smell the acrid cordite from the bullet, as if he'd just pulled the trigger on his pistol. His pistol, how he wished he'd got it now!

"Then if I shot-a you, how-a...?" his voice trailed off as he watched the Cat sit up and lick a paw. Budleigh could clearly see the bullet hole in her chest.

"How can I be here, alive, licking my paws?"

"Yes-a!" exclaimed a spooked Budleigh.

"You would be surprised what I can do," replied the Cat. Standing up, she reached a hooked paw toward the top of the jar and began to fish for Budleigh.

Budleigh started running around inside the vase, bobbing and weaving, trying to avoid Amelia's grasp. He flattened himself on the floor of the jar, but the Cat just reached deeper. While massive to Budleigh, the Cat was actually quite small by Purpolian standards. She began to tilt the jar towards her. The jar now was almost at the angle of no return. Frantically, Budleigh scrambled backwards up the rapidly sloping floor, his feet slipping under him on the smooth glass.

The Cat's paw hunted for him, dabbing around, narrowly missing his trouser leg. The Cat strained at the opening, "Another few inches," she thought, stretching her leg a little further. The nasty little cat killer was now within reach.

Budleigh felt the jar beginning to topple forward and saw his chance of escape. He waited until the Cat's paw touched the bottom of the glass, and, stepping on the top of it, he ran up the Cat's leg and out of the top of the jar. He was free!

It was at this point, he spotted the flaw in his otherwise flawless plan. He was running straight into the Cat's open mouth, which it had helpfully placed directly into Budleigh's path!

"Amelia! What are you doing?" came a voice from across the room. Budleigh toppled into Amelia's mouth, which snapped shut, trapping him from the waist up. Budleigh's legs kicked and thrashed, his elbows battered at the inside of her incisors, his senses too horrified to acknowledge the rough tongue he'd landed on. The Cat was about to turn and run, when, from above, two giant black hands swept Amelia from the floor and high into the air.

Garvandulan had a tight hold of Amelia and could hear a very unhappy and somewhat muffled Budleigh, cursing and cussing from within the Cat's jaws.

"Time to let go now Amelia," said Garvandulan, as he grasped Budleigh's legs and started pulling at them. What followed was a quite unseemly tussle between the Cat and Garvandulan, first pulling this way, then that, a tug-o-war with Budleigh as the rope! He was in danger of being sawn in half by her scissor-sharp teeth.

"Amelia! Let him go, he is my guest!" insisted Spang. Garvandulan changed tactics and began to gently tickle her ears. She was so surprised, she let go of Budleigh, whipping her head to the left. Garvandulan hadn't expected this to work quite so well or quite so quickly; Budleigh was catapulted across the room like an angry, shouty stuffed toy.

"Arrrrgggghhh-a!" he cried, as he flipped through the air ."Whooooooah-a!" he shrieked, as he desperately scanned the on-rushing earth, to try to work out where his likely impact point was going to be. "Gerrrrrrrrk-" The final "a" never came, as Budleigh crashed, head first, into a giant-sized pile of thickly cut ham sandwiches.

For a few seconds, he didn't move. Landing on your head is a hard thing to do once a day, let alone twice!

When Budleigh finally gathered his thoughts, he pulled his head out from the bread, righted himself and sat among the sarnies. He reached into the hole his head had made in the bread and pulled out his doubly battered hat. It was folded, like the pleats of an accordion, and covered in butter and mustard: he didn't bother straightening it this time, instead just plonking it back on top of his head and reached out for a chunk of sandwich. "Ham-a sandwiches! Mmmm....!" he exclaimed, before promptly passing out.

Chapter 10

Scooping up Budleigh, Garvandulan put him back in the jar and then into a sturdy glass-fronted cabinet, locking it behind him and slipping the key into his waistcoat pocket.

"Garvandulan, let me have him. It's only fair. He did shoot me after all." The Cat wound herself around his leg as she wheedled away at him. "I'll make it quick and almost painless..." around and around she went. "What's one tiny man to you?"

Spang shot the Cat a withering look. "My dear Amelia, we do not eat the guests, no matter how much they may have shot you in the past. How are we to encourage them to change if all we do is exact revenge? Where will that get us, hmmm?"

"A great sense of satisfaction and a full belly, that's where!" Despite Amelia being fifty percent Boggis, she was also fifty percent cat and that was the part that was telling her to eat Budleigh.

"We won't be eating anything other than the delicious meal I'll be serving you up later. Now be off with you, I've to take Mr Salterton and Rexford to see the Prime Minister!" Amelia knew better than to meddle in the Prime Minister's business, for as kind as Garvandulan was, the PM was an entirely different bucket of giblets. She slunk out of the kitchen and into the garden outside.

"Right, let's get you ready," Spang spoke into the air. "Now where is Rexford?" Reaching into his pocket he felt for the rat who, incredibly, was still asleep, curled up next to the key. Carefully scooping him up, he eyed the round rat. Rexford began to rouse.

"Two sugars, extra bacon and toast please Six." Two thirds asleep, Rexford thought he was still in the turret, Six ready to bring him his breakfast.

"Will a ham sandwich do?"

Rexford struggled to his feet and gazed out over the giant's thumb. No, this wasn't the castle. His eye swivelled about trying to latch on to something he recognised. No, nothing yet, nope, still nothing, wait - was that Budleigh? In a jar? In a cabinet? Hat covered in mustard? What was going on here?!

He opened the other eye and looked at the ground below him.

Except that wasn't the ground. It looked very much like the palm of a very large hand. A large hand, belonging to a very large arm, which belonged to an even larger man, who was staring directly at him.

"Gerk and good morning Rexford. I trust you slept well."

"Yes I had a lovely sleep actua... " Rexford never finished the sentence. He shook his head vigorously and gathered his thoughts very rapidly. "What is going on and why is Budleigh covered in mustard in a jar? Are you going to eat us?" Rexford cowered slightly at the thought of him being the filling for an oversized finger roll.

"No, no no," Spang replied. "No, I'm taking you to see the Prime Minister. We need to give you a wash and brush up." The giant threw a flannel to Rexford, that to him was the size of a large beach towel. "Take that dirty dress off and I'll give it a wash for you."

"This is not a dress, sir, it is my nightshirt. I have no dresses with me!"

"Well, whatever it is, give it to me so that I may wash it."

Rexford removed his night clothes and wrapped the flannel about himself.

"Good!" said the giant. "Now have a wash." He lowered Rexford into the sink and turned the tap on, just a bit. Warm water cascaded down from the tap as a makeshift shower, which Rex gladly got under.

"Got any shampoo?" he enquired. Spang briefly disappeared. On his return he was carrying a thimble full of a frothy liquid. "Excellent!" Rexford began to lather his fur, which was actually quite grubby after all he'd been through. His face was particularly greasy as he'd discovered the hard way, night cream doesn't suit rats. He worked his way around himself paying special attention to his tail, which was always getting dragged through something or another. He lent down and took an exploratory lick, on this particular occasion, it was butter. He was tempted to carry on licking, but was aware of being watched, so sung a hesitant, half whistled, half croaked version of a song he'd made up on the long evenings at the castle. He sang it to the tune of 'Ring a Ring o' Roses'.

I am going to be King

Of absolutely everything,
Bless me, bless me
You're all going down.

I am so amazing
At running gangs and lazing,
Going up, going up
While Basil comes down.

It was a bit of a dream, given his current circumstances, but cheered him up when he was feeling lost. Rexford hadn't got very far with his song writing career, but felt he had more to offer.

Ten minutes later he was finished and stepped out of the shower, into the flannel, patting himself dry as he went. Whilst he had been at his ablutions, Garvandulan washed his clothes. He wrung the white nightie out over the sink and set it next to the stove to dry.

"What are we going to do with you, Mr Salterton?" He looked at the crumpled heap, that was the battered Bud. Budleigh looked like he'd never had an actual bath or even a spit, lick and wipe from an over-anxious aunty before. In fact if you were to try to bath Mr Salterton, there stood a good chance that there would be nothing left of him by the time you'd finished, so ingrained was the dirt.

"I'll have to do something - he can't meet the PM looking like that!" Budleigh was, fortunately, still out for the count. Garvandulan walked up to the dresser and reached inside his pocket for the key. He unlocked the cabinet, removed the vase containing Budleigh and placed it on the draining board next to the sink. Spang reached inside the jar and hauled Budleigh out. "My my, what a mess."

Spang took another flannel and began his attempt at cleaning Budleigh up. He'd nearly finished wiping the butter and mustard from Budleigh's hat, when he started to come round. "Better be quick," thought Garvandulan and he wiped and polished the dirty herbert as best he could. He took a fresh jar and placed the appreciably cleaner Mr Salterton back into it.

Rexford's night frock had dried and he returned it to Rex, who slipped it on and sat down, positively glowing. Taking a step back, the giant surveyed his two charges. "That's better! Now you're ready to see the Prime Minister!" He gathered them up, tucking Budleigh's jar under his arm and stashing Rex back in his pocket. "We must go now. We don't want to keep the PM waiting, do we?"

Garvandulan Spang headed to the door, locking it behind him, "Come on Amelia, you're coming too," he called over to the curled cat, as he loped off through the jungle toward the centre of Purpolis.

Chapter 11

As the crow flies, it's not too far to the centre of Purpolis from Garvandulan's house, but it seems a lot further than it actually is, due to its ridiculously narrow streets. For some reason, known only to themselves, the Purpolians had, rather obtusely, decided to build a city that was far too small for them. The streets were incredibly narrow, so that when one Purpolian passed another Purpolian, it required them both to flatten themselves against opposite walls and edge past each other, whilst constantly apologising for their ancestors' lack of foresight and town planning.

Every part of the city was like this. Getting supplies and goods in and out was a nightmare, so much so, that the residents had constructed an incredibly elaborate system of towers, wires and pulleys to help speed up the transport of things around the city.

Unfortunately, all it actually did was hopelessly complicate matters as, to maintain some kind of order, each delivery had to be highly coordinated months in advance, to avoid mid-air collisions - such as the Great Aubergine Debacle, in which a consignment of tennis racquets had crashed into the city's year's supply of highly valuable aubergines, shredding the entire load.

Although the Purpolians were vegan by inclination, they only ate purple food out of necessity. The compounds that made the food purple also helped keep them healthy.

The small blue sun they lived under tended to emit a lot of ultraviolet light, which could set off free radicals in their bodies and skin. The purpleness in the vegetables combated this and helped keep them in good health, when otherwise they might quickly fall ill. Losing an entire year's supply of aubergines, was nothing short of a disaster.

That is, until someone noticed that when the tennis racquets' gutty grid smashed into the delicious purple plant, they had behaved like hundreds of potato chippers and had turned the entire crop into neat rectangular cuboids. As luck would have it, some of the pieces fell directly into a bowl of heated vegetable oil the Purpolians used to grease the axles of the pulleys that kept the overhead delivery system functioning. In that moment, when chip'o'gine met hot oil, deep fat frying was born and no one ever ate another boiled aubergine again.

Coincidentally, the person responsible for maintaining this hideously complicated system was Garvandualan Spang. It was so important to the Purpolians, the Head of the Skyhookerator always had unfettered access to the Prime Minister of the day, and so it was, that Garvandulan Spang lumbered up the stairs of the PM's official Residence, 10 Drowning Street.

It was called Drowning Street because it was the only part of Purpolia that was below sea level and it would flood on a semi-regular basis. Someone once suggested moving the location of the official residence to the only hill in Purpolia, as the disruption caused when Drowning Street flooded took months to sort out. In bad years, they would not finish the restorations before it would flood and they'd have to start all over again.

The Prime Minister of the day had had the person who suggested moving banished to the furthest ends of the land, because when the official residence flooded, it meant the PM had to go to the Prime Minister's Official Retreat (PMOR), which was a straw covered hut in the middle of the warm and calm Purpolian Sea. There was no easy way to contact the PM and there was room service - so the incentive to fix Drowning Street was not really there, to be honest.

However, on this occasion, Drowning Street was dry and Spang knocked on the door.

"Hello," came a small voice from inside. "Who is it?"

"Garvandulan," he said regally, glancing at the Cat.

"Who?" said the voice.

"Garvandulan Spang. Let me in." Garvandulan looked around awkwardly. A small crowd had started to gather.

"Garbalisham Sponge? And who's the hairy fella with you?" queried the voice.

"Garvandulan Spang. Head of the Skyhookerator!" Spang was becoming irritated now, "and Amelia the Cat."

"Oh," said the voice.

There was a pause.

"Never heard of you."

Spang banged on the door with his fist. The crowd had started to giggle. "He can't get in," one of them muttered.

Then someone else shouted "Now you know what it's like trying to book a hook!" (as they called the Skyhookerator booking procedure).

Spang banged again.

"Who is it?" came the voice.

"OPEN THIS DOOR!" hissed Spang.

"Ok," said the voice. "You only had to ask."

Garvandulan entered and brushed the doorkeeper aside. "Still no idea who you are," she muttered, as Spang sped off down a long corridor, the Cat bounding along beside him, toward the Prime Minister's apartments.

Knocking once more, Garvandulan let out a big sigh and slumped against the wall. This time, the door swung open to reveal the Prime Minister of Purpolia, sitting at a desk, munching at a large bowl of aubergine chips.

"Hello Garvandulan," she said. "Want a chip?"

The Prime Minister of Purpolia was a very old, almost regal, position. It takes ten years of continual elections to determine the outcome of a General Election. This is quite consistent with the Purpolian's love of the obtuse and awkward.

Of the ten years of continuous voting, only one ballot actually matters, but no one knows which one it is, so as a consequence, everyone votes in every election, so as to be sure not to lose their vote.

The elections are held every Sunday, in the most congested

part of Purpolia, at the end of Drowning Street. Sometimes, when it rains and Drowning Street floods, elections can go on for years longer than the ten year minimum. The current occupant of the role of Prime Minister had taken thirteen years to be elected. The upside of the rigorous election system, was that the holder enjoyed the position for life, or until everyone got bored, whichever came first.

"Prime Minister, I have something quite wonderful to show you. Something brought to my door by the Crabbage. They were scared when they found them on the shore and decided to bring them to me. I have fed and cleaned them, as you will see. May I present," he paused for effect, "Mr Salterton and Rexford." With a flourish, Garvandulan took the jar from under his arm and shook Budleigh out on the desk: he landed on his head for the third time that day.

"Ouch-a!" a half-hearted Budleigh groaned.

Reaching into his pocket, he pulled the glowing Rexford out and set him down next to Budleigh. "Good day," announced Overstreet. "And who might you be?"

The Prime Minister nearly dropped her chip in surprise. "What are these? Automata? Clockwork toys? They seem to speak. Are they real?"

"As far as I can tell, Prime Minister. They eat, sleep and make quite a bit of fuss if the Cat gets hold of them. So yes, I would say they are."

"Where did they come from?"

"I'm not really sure. As I said, the Crabbage brought them to me, so I'm assuming they were washed ashore from a far-off land."

Amelia's eyes were level with the edge of the desk and she stared at Budleigh intently. She knew where they were from all right and she hadn't given up on sorting Salterton out.

"Incredible!" said Perpetual Dawn, the Prime Minister of Purpolia, clapping her hands together. All Prime Ministers of Purpolia had the title of Perpetual as, once elected, they tended to hang around. Perpetual Dawn was preceded by Perpetual Eric, who was in turn preceded by Perpetual Prudence. The only exception to this was the first PM of Purpolia, Temporary Trudy, who really didn't want the job in the first place, but had a go whilst the tortuous Election process went on to find her successor. It was also Temporary Trudy who located her official residence in Drowning Street and who had set up the Official Retreat.

Fortunately\unfortunately for Temporary Trudy, she died the day Perpetual Dominic was finally elected to the job, proving to be truly worthy of her name.

"Little People! How strange. H-e-l-l-o-l-i-t-t-l-e-p-e-o-p-l-e. W-h-a-t-a-r-e-y-o-u-r-n-a-m-e-s?" She was speaking as she would to someone who was slightly hard of hearing.

"W-h-y-a-r-e-y-o-u-s-p-e-a-k-i-n-g-l-i-ke-t-h-a-t?" Rexford mouthed back.

"Prime Minister," ventured Spang, "they can hear you just as you can hear me. They have a greeting. 'Gerk.' Try this."

"Gurk?" she attempted.

"No, Gerk, Prime Minister."

"Gerk. Little people!" She held up the palm of her right hand, supposedly in greeting, although she had never felt the need to do this before. "What are you doing here in our land of Purpolia?"

Rexford took a step forward, with his hands clasped behind his back. "Well you see, we're not really sure. There was a room, a white room, and then we fell a long way and found ourselves on a strange beach." He was beginning to warm to his theme. He leaned in a gave small 'come closer' gesture. The PM and Spang craned their necks and leaned in closer. Conspiratorially, Rexford continued, "Well, between you and me, wherever we are, it's much better than prison..." His voice trailed off as the faces of his hosts promptly dropped. "Too much information?" he winced.

Budleigh, who was now fully back in the room, glared at Rexford. "Rex-a, Rex-a," he hissed. "Shut up-a!" But it was too late. The damage was done.

"Prison? Prison! You are escaped prisoners? Garvandulan Spang what *were* you thinking of, bringing common criminals in to centre of government? You know how we deal with criminals in Purpolia!" Perpetual Dawn rounded on Bud and Rex. "What did you do that made you into prisoners?"

Budleigh clapped a hand over Rexford's open mouth before he had a chance to say anymore. "Well-a you see, Prime Minister-a , it was a terrible injustice-a that led-a to our incarceration. We were-a framed-a by a big headed rodent-a and a girl. Why my-a associate and I-a could never harm-a a living soul-a."

"You murdered me!" said a large pair of unblinking eyes at the end of the desk, "and I've got the bullet hole to prove it."

"Is this true, Amelia?" asked Perpetual Dawn.

"Very," said the Cat, who was standing on the desk and edging ever closer to Budleigh.

"Oh-a that-a. That-a was a misunderstanding-a."

"It didn't feel like it," said the Cat as she looked down and parted her fur to reveal the bullet hole, "Nope, there's the hole, clean through, fired from your pistol, Budleigh Salterton."

"Well done Budleigh old chap, that's made everything much better!" said Rexford as Budleigh relaxed his grasp.

"Well, this all seems pretty straight forward," continued Dawn. "Justice must be served and, even though your crime wasn't committed here, you must still pay. Little people or not, you will be taken to jail, while we prepare a trial for you. Garvandulan, book an emergency hook and take these two to jail immediately."

Immediately and 'booking a hook' didn't go together well, as there was such demand that any disruption would cause riots later on. The best he could do was to see if there was a delivery going to the jail and get these two on as excess baggage. Spang left the room for a moment, to organise transport.

"I could help transport them Prime Minister. I could have them there in no time," Amelia was wheedling again. "Better than disrupting the deliveries. You know how annoyed everyone gets...."

"That's not a bad idea, Amelia. Can you manage them both?"

"Oh yes, Prime Minister. I can carry them in my mouth." She was now staring very intently at Budleigh, who was starting to perspire. Amelia licked her lips, bared her razor sharp teeth and took a half step forward. Budleigh let out a strangled squeal, "Eeek-a!"

Just as he was preparing to be eaten, out of the corner of one eye, Budleigh noticed something on the floor of the office. Could it be? Keeping one eye on the advancing cat, he looked again. My goodness, can it be? Yes it was. His Gladstone Bag, just by the edge of the desk!

The Cat was almost on him, grabbing Rexford, he shoved his fellow criminal directly at the Cat, which gave him just enough time to make a break for it and dive head first into his bag.

The Cat, who wasn't as interested in Rexford, batted him away and made for the bag. Fortunately for Rex, the Cat had swiped him toward the open bag and his momentum carried him on over the edge of the desk; there he followed Budleigh into the Gladstone bag, which promptly snapped shut behind him.

While they both expected to hit the bottom of the bag fairly swiftly, they did not. In fact they were now falling again. This time they fell down. Down, down, down they fell.

"Here we go again!" mouthed Rex to Bud, as they fell to who-knew-where.

Chapter 12

Who put the bag there and why was it so big? Or rather, how had they come to be so small? And was it even a bag? It certainly didn't feel much like a bag at the moment. It felt more like a void, a big black void, through which they were both falling downwards this time, but to where, or what?

As they fell, Budleigh shouted to Rexford, "Bangle. What are-a we going to do-a about Bangle-a?"

"What?" Rexford shouted back. "What do you mean? What can we do about Bangle? He seems to know our thoughts before we've even had them, and, to be honest with you old man, I'm not even sure what he is. He doesn't seem to have a definite form. He seems to wobble about quite a bit!"

"Whilst he's-a free-a, we won't-a be-a! He's-a playing with us-a Rex. All the falling-a, the giants-a, the bag-a and, worst of all-a, the Cat!" screamed Budleigh. The wind was really whooshing past them now. "He's-a always going to be after us-a, poking his nose in-a, whenever he feels-a like it. We need-a to get him!"

"Get him? Whatever do you mean?" Cord Bangle wasn't even from this dimension and he could read minds, stop time and freeze you mid-jump! "Getting him isn't an option," Rexford huffed, although it was a good idea in theory, and he wished he'd thought of it himself.

Neither of them seemed to notice the onrushing ground, they were so wrapped up in their thoughts. They came to a screaming halt exactly 0.0000001mm above its surface, leaving them to fall exactly 0.0000001mm to the ground.

In fact, they were so accustomed to the falling now that for them, it had become a little like stepping out of a lift.

At first, they barely noticed a thin grey mist enveloping them - thin, but seemingly impenetrable. Budleigh blinked and looked again. "What fresh-a hell is this-a?" he snarled aloud."Do your worst-a, there's nothing left to break-a!" he shouted into the air.

He looked again, straining into the murk, like a terrified sailor on watch in iceberg alley, until he fancied he could see faces in the distance: beautiful, ugly, old, young, all looking pleadingly, as if they wanted something.

He blinked and refocused. They seemed to be moving toward him through a greyness so intense, it was like a criss-cross pattern of gossamer fibres, a giant web. He gulped and looked again. The faces were getting larger, more insistent, they seemed to be floating. "Floating heads?" he murmured, surprised, even though he didn't think anything could ever surprise him again.

The faces floated closer and closer. Pleading eyes focused on him, him, him. Suddenly, he could hear them. At first it was a rhythmic silvery whisper, like a warm wind blowing through an acacia tree on a vast African plain, hot and soporific. He suddenly felt drowsy, as they loomed through the gloom. Closer, the noise rose to meet him, mutating into a jarring caterwaul, a great discordant cacophony, every pitch, from highest soprano to lowest bass. He clapped his hands over his ears and stared, wide-eyed. Fear found and squeezed him. It started in his chest and spread through his arms and fingers and all the way down to his toes. Still they came. Lips mouthing wordless words, teeth flashing. From out of nowhere, arms appeared, hands outstretched, fingers pointing, stretching out towards him. Closer, closer. Touching!

Budleigh screwed his eyes shut and pressed his hands even more tightly over his ears. He opened his mouth and let out a long anguished cry, that almost became one with the noise.

Abruptly, he stopped wailing and opened his eyes. Budleigh was in a grey room. He looked for the faces, the floating heads, but they were gone. Was that good? Was he alone? He felt a pang of solitude. Budleigh feared loneliness, which was quite surprising considering how he behaved most of the time.

Being Budleigh's friend was a job no one had ever passed the interview for. In fact, no one had ever applied for the post in the first place! A salivary murmur from somewhere beside him caught him off guard.

"Rexford!" Budleigh felt relieved. Even though he and Rex could hardly be described as friends, they did share this common experience. No one could possibly understand what had happened to him except Rex. His relief at finding himself accompanied, soon turned to horror.

"What godforsaken place is this-a now?" he rasped at Rexford. The rat lay panting on his back and didn't respond. For a moment, Budleigh was concerned about him. He instantly regretted it, when Rexford struggled to a seating position, clutching his head.

"Ooo My head! What was all the shouting about?"

"What-a? Didn't you see-a the heads-a? The floating screaming-a heads? The hands-a? The grabbing hands-a?"

"All I saw was you, careering around, wherever we are, making an awful racket, until you caught me on the side of the head with your knee, which nearly knocked me out! We really must be more careful with our consciousness, we can't keep losing it like this!"

....

A great whiteness descends. A whiteness like the inside of a cloud but with less fluff. A whiteness so complete and all enveloping, Budleigh and Rexford can't tell up from down or left from right. "Grey never looked so good," Rexford muses, when a slight change, a wrinkle in the light, makes him look up. Budleigh's eyes join his. They both wish they were looking somewhere else, for a smiling floating head slowly comes into view, revealing itself like a coin exposing the numbers on a scratch card.

"Now now gentlemen, what's all this noise about?" says Cord Bangle, finding arms and legs from somewhere and arranging them about him in the whiteness, in a way that is almost visible to the dirty duo.
"Who the hell-a do you think-a you are-a?" Budleigh snarls, "and where the hell-a is this-a?"
"I'm sorry, I'll not have that tone of voice here!" Cord returns.
"Where am I-a?" demands Budleigh again.
"My good man," Cord continues. "When you can stop with the snarling and demanding, we can talk. Until then...." and with that, he disappears back into the cloud and is gone.

Budleigh was staring once again at the greyness. He cursed under his breath.

"Well done Salteron, you buffoon! That might have been our way out of here!"

"Shut up-a rodent!" he hissed at Rexford and then more quietly, "Shut up-a."

He hated being told what to do. However, even he realised Rexford was probably right, so he resolved to try and control his temper if Bangle came back.

....

After a minute, or an hour, or a day - they couldn't be sure of anything in this place - a familiar whiteness settles once more over the grey.

Budleigh sits up straight, as Cord's face develops like a negative in a darkroom. "Is there any-a chance of you taking us home-a?" he asks, in what he hopes is a very respectful and endearing tone.

"Home?" echoes Bangle. "Where would you be calling home, old chap? The cabin in the wood? The castle? The open road...?"

As Cord lists the places Budleigh has called home, images appear, shimmering behind him, colourfully, vibrantly shocking, as they contrast with the disorientating, enveloping whiteness. Both Budleigh and Rexford are transfixed by the images, so vivid they almost seem real.

Rex reaches out to touch the scenes before him.

"No touching," Cord instructs.

Rexford withdraws his paw, as if slapped. "A word is worth a thousand pictures," he mumbles, to no one in particular.

As the images appear before them, Budleigh recognises the rough wooden cabin. It is his childhood home. His grandfather had built it many years before and when the old man died, his mother, father and an infant Budleigh ad gone to live there. It has largely remained as it had been when his grandfather was alive, except for the curtains his mother had so painstakingly made: little blue and white flowers, scattered over cream cotton, that swayed and billowed in the breeze, like flowers in a field. Budleigh feels a pang in his heart as he looks at them.

Now there are figures appearing, as if they are stepping out of a painting. He gasps, "Mother!" Budleigh feels a lump rise in his throat. "Mother." All of a sudden, from somewhere in the shadows, a hand is placed on his mother's shoulder. Budleigh narrows his eyes, straining to see to whom the hand belongs. He jumps backwards in shock and disbelief. His father steps forward, looks straight at Budleigh and gives the unmistakable Salterton broken-toothed grin. Budleigh is extremely shaken by this sudden spectre. The scene quickly fades and the castle appears. He is surrounded by deranged mechanical men dancing and prancing.

Ashen-faced at the sight of his long-dead father, Budleigh barks "No!" before catching himself. He changes the subject of his objection, quickly before anyone notices. "No please-a, not the castle. What do you want-a from us-a?"

"Well gentleman, what do I want? What do I want?" cries Cord Bangle imperiously. "What I want is a modicum of gratitude, a little bit of respect, a little praise and understanding. Am I not helpful? Am I not kind? Have I not spared your lives, too many times, when I could have crushed you like peppercorns into gravy, like peanuts into butter? You two gentlemen are becoming peskier than the peskiest pesks and ungrateful into the bargain!"

Budleigh's instinct is to shout at this ridiculous glowing white man, but he knows better. Rexford, too, knows how to fawn.

"I say again, I save your pitiful lives when less generous souls would have crushed you, provide an all-expenses-paid relaxing break in the finest castle in the land, but are you grateful? Are you heck!" Bangle starts to pace back and forth, washing through the waves of whiteness.

"I even fix it for you to have a holiday in the sun with my old chum Garvandulan, hoping you may see the error of your ways, if only you have some time to think about it and reflect on what you've done."

"What have-a we done-a?" interjects Budleigh, he'd been frozen at the time and had actually missed this conversation at the castle.

"Overstreet, tell him!" Cord orders.

Rexford plays dumb, fiddling furiously with the hem of his nightshirt.

"Well? I'm waiting!"

"Kidnapping, unlawful incarceration, assault and battery, theft and treason."

"Pardon?"

"Kidnapping, unlawful incarceration, assault and battery, theft and treason."

"Sorry?"

"Kidnapping, unlawful incarceration, assault and battery, theft and treason."

Budleigh's eyes widen, but he has the sense to keep quiet.

"And what are you?"

"I'm a double-crossing, lying, cheating bully who would sell his own grandmother for a bacon sandwich. I am bad from the soles of my paws to the tips of my whiskers."

....

Barely had he got the words out, when Rexford found himself transported to an alien place. A dark place. A place alone. He wasn't standing on solid ground, but bobbing in the ether.

"What now?" he muttered to himself. As he said this, a small point of light appeared just beyond his reach. The point hovered there for a moment, before stretching into a long vertical line. The long vertical shaft of light now stretched again, this time it transformed along the horizontal, to form a large floating rectangle of pure light.

"Oh my..." said Rex. The rectangle of light pulsed gently before him, before it started to twitch and glitch into life, until it became an image of his ten year old self looking out of his bedroom window.

Rexford stopped wondering about his surroundings and, instead, fully concentrated on the flickering images of his life hovering before him...

As Rexford watched, he could see his younger self begin to start throwing coins from his bedroom window at a young rat, who was perched on the steps of his mansion.

"What was that?" thought the young Sniffer, for it was he, and he turned to see where the coin had come from.

Sniffer McGurk was an unlikely villain. He fell in with Rexford's gang almost by accident. Mrs McGurk had had a lot of children. Most of Sniffer's brothers and sisters had gone to work for Bradley Overstreet in his scrapyards, finding and sorting the scrap metals that had made Bradley rich. But Sniffer was a sickly little thing, with a permanently runny nose, hence his nickname. He had been too weak to haul the heavy scrap around and would sit on the steps of Overstreet Manor instead, waiting for his siblings to finish their daily toil. He would do this come rain or shine, which would only make his runny nose worse. From a lonely bedroom, a bored little Rexford watched Sniffer sitting on the step.

'Whizz-thock!' Sniffer felt the sting of a missile, launched from behind, hit him on the back of the neck.

"Ouch!" he yelled.

'Whizz-ptang!' Another projectile just missed his ear and ricocheted off the step beside him. He turned to see where the bombs were coming from.

'Whizz-peaow.' Another smashed a flowerpot to his left. Looking up, he saw a ringletted rat in a sailor suit launch another coin in his direction.

"Stop it!" he yelled up at the window.

"Why should I?" came the reply.

"It hurts," shouted Sniffer, now on his feet and dodging the continuing onslaught.

"So what? It's funny!" guffawed Rexford.

"No it's not, it hurts!"

"It doesn't hurt me. It makes me laugh!"

"Come down here and say that!" said Sniffer, who instantly regretted it when Rexford disappeared from the window and, almost immediately, reappeared by his side.

Rexford was a good deal taller and fatter than Sniffer. All the excitement had set off his runny nose. Two candles made their way down his face and onto his threadbare shirt.

"What's the matter with you? Don't you own a handkerchief?"

Sniffer didn't, unless you could count his shirt sleeves. He just looked at Rexford. The two couldn't be any more different.

"Do you want to be in my gang?" Rexford asked.

"Gang?" replied a puzzled Sniffer.
"Yes, I'm starting a gang and we're going to be called the Mischiefs, you know, like the film?"

Rexford blinked. The window closed. Sniffer was gone.

The ordeal wasn't over yet. The point of light reappeared, twanging tantalisingly just to his left. It hovered there for an instant, playing with him. Rexford watched it like a child looking at bubbles blown from a stick, his mouth in the shape of an 'O'. He stood still, waiting, panting.

The point of light suddenly made up its mind, stretched into a vertical line, and now, with impressive resolve, sprung into a large screen of scintillating, pixelated white.

Rexford blinked, the brightness making him squint. The little dots danced and swam about, linking together, breaking apart, fizzing like lemonade. The purity of the screen made his eyes ache, but he couldn't look away. He blinked again and found himself seated at a wooden table with high sides. On the table was a glass of water, some blank pages and a rather old looking quill pen. Looking up, he gasped. Opposite him a row of eyes glared from faces, attached to a row of bodies he recognised.

Rexford gulped. Seated in the middle of a sweeping circular bench was Basil!

"Oh Lord. Well if it isn't The Most Excellent Count Basilimous Horattus Bevelonious the Third of Upp-"

"Silence!" Basil barked. Rexford saw seated to his right, Monty and Pearl Peppersquerl, their daughter Porcelaina, Si Speriment and Basil's wife Kitty; to his left, The Cat, Budleigh Salterton, 'Sniffer' McGurk, 'Three Fingers' Smith, 'Cringer' Wilson and Colin the bear.

"You are accused of kidnapping, unlawful incarceration, assault and battery, theft and treason How do you plead?" shouted Basil.

Rexford looked around him. He was now standing as the accused, in a wooden dock, he shut his eyes again and opened them in his own underground laboratory, his guards stood outside the door. "Open this door immediately!" he yelled. The guards didn't seem to hear. "Let me out, you idiots!" Rexford bawled. "Do you know who I am!" He banged and shouted till his lungs and knuckles were in tatters, before sliding down the wall into a crumpled, hopeless heap on the rough ground.

He blinked again, Rexford was now in his control room in Lower Rattopia. The screens that normally flickered about him were dark, as he sat alone listening to the sounds of the night. Darkness stole around him, seeping into his bones, a malevolent degenerate darkness, thief of even the tiniest chink of light. He wasn't sure if he'd been there for an hour or a month. He could feel his heartbeat throbbing in his ears and wondered how he'd ever gone from playing golf in his plus fours, brogues, checked waistcoat and flat cap, to being here, sucked into a void of unreality, cold, alone and afraid, wearing nothing but his nightie, washed for him by a kind giant in a purple land with a purple sky and a tiny blue sun.

"It's just a nightmare," Rexford said to himself. "Just a nightmare!" He screwed his eyes tight and resolved to keep them shut.

It didn't work. A minute later he was manacled to a damp wall. Dripping water seeped into his fur. His wrists ached and smarted. The tight metal of heavy shackles cut into his skin. A lit torch flickered from its holster and shed just enough light for him to see that he was imprisoned in his own dungeon.

He shut his eyes and opened them in a wood. An enormous

brown bear looked down at him. "Where do you live?" the bear asked.

"I can't remember," Rexford answered.
"Oh, haven't you got a home?" the bear laughed, disappearing into the bushes.

"This isn't real!" Rexford told himself. "It isn't real." He could smell burning. Si Speriment stood in the remains of his house, looking pathetically up at him. He held out a singed clump of wet and blackened papers, "My life's work" he cried. "My life's work!"

"And the star witness," shouted Basil. "Call Sol Gilberta Hunter."

A good looking boy was led into the middle of the arena. He looked at the ground when he saw Rexford, flinching away from him with the practiced shrug of the long abused.

"Is this the dirty rat who kept you beaten and half starved, working as his slave for the best part of fifteen years?"

The boy looked up through his thick fringe. The jury caught the wince of recognition in his face. "Confirmed! Confirmed!" Basil yelled, banging his gavel hard on the bench, before the boy had had a chance to speak.

A silent tear ran down Gilberta's face. Rexford moved towards the terrified boy and stretched a paw out to calm him.

The boy morphed into a man, a tall man, wearing a large black leather coat that touched the ground, a black shirt and trousers with a large black belt, crossed silver pistols and crowned with a top hat, a black crow feather jammed into the brim, pointed to the heavens.

"Why-a you snivelling little-a double crosser," Budleigh Salterton hissed, through his remaining teeth. He bent down snarling, nose to nose with Rexford. "You-a really thought-a you could steal-a that ungrateful-a little madam, my hamma sandwich stealer, from clean under my nose-a!" As he spoke, the green, yellow, and blue glass beads rattled on the end of his thin beard, and his breath, sharp and repugnant, swept around Rexford's face. He leaned further down, placed both gloved hands around his neck and started to squeeze, a silver ring digging into Rexford's windpipe.

"Have you had enough yet, Overstreet?" shouted Basil, but Rexford couldn't hear him. Budleigh kept snarling and pressing, pressing and snarling, louder, louder and louder. He clamped his paws over his ears.

"Make it stop! Make it stop, Horratus!"

"How do you plead?"

"Guilty! I'm guilty and I'm sorry."

Rexford closes his eyes and opens them again. Nothing has moved. Cord Bangle looms above him.

"Well what do you think, Overstreet? Pleasant viewing it does not make, eh?"

In silence, Rexford shrugs his shoulders and stares at the ground. Following this experience, something changes in him and not in the way Cord had anticipated. Something

breaks inside Rexford, and not in a good way.
Budleigh Salterton stands unsure on his feet, next to him, looking up, slightly pitifully, at Cord's omnipresent face.

"And you, Budleigh Salterton," the face says, "have an even longer list of crimes, to which I believe I can add the despicable act of double murder!" Cord slows down at the end of the sentence for added emphasis.

Silence seeps into the whiteness and settles between them.
....

Budleigh called it 'the incident' because it was too painful for him to focus on entirely. He could remember bits of it, corners and angles, but never the full horrific picture in one go.

At first, a single point of light appeared, just out of reach before him. Then it became a vertical line, then a large glowing rectangle. It skipped and flickered into life.

He had now been given a ringside seat at the re-run of the horror story that was his life. He was no coward, but Bangle could not have dealt him a harder blow if he'd clubbed him round the head with a brick. He tried to shut his eyes, but a force he didn't understand cranked them open, wider every time, until he was forced to watch, painfully clearly, the lighted scroll of pictures play out before him.

Chapter 13

A young Budleigh skipped excitedly up and down the stairs with his new puppy. The tiny white whippet nestled under his arm and whimpered slightly. Budleigh was a kind child. As soon as he realised his pet was uncomfortable, he rushed to put him down in his new bed - a basket he'd lined with moss from the wood behind his parents' cabin. He petted and fussed over the little dog, then covered him with a blanket until just the tip of his black nose was peeking out.

His mother sung as she wound the last ringlet of her hair onto her head. "Ready?" she called. Budleigh wasn't a great fan of school, but it meant he had his mother to himself for twenty minutes every morning, as they walked hand in hand through the wood to his makeshift classroom. Calling it a school may have been a bit of an overstatement, for it was only a corrugated iron hut, with three rows of wooden benches, a blackboard, an old piano and a few textbooks. Mrs James did her best with meagre resources and her six pupils. Most days, Budleigh had a good kick around with a ball, at break, with her son Thomas.

"Coming!" Seven year old Budleigh took the stairs two at a time and rushed to his mother's side. She smiled down warmly at the boy clutching her hand. There had been times when she had despaired, black miserable days stretching out before her, when she had lost hope of ever having a child, but then, at her bleakest moment, she had felt small stirrings inside her, which she hadn't dared to recognise until her rounded belly spoke for itself.

....

Salterton Senior doted on his wife. He spent his time attending to her needs and wondering how he'd ever got so lucky. He was more than a little surprised to find he had a son. He feigned pleasure when the bundle of boy was placed in his arms, and smiled at his delighted wife, but an unfamiliar feeling was stirring in his heart.

Budleigh and his mother walked their usual route through the forest, Grace steering the child skillfully round stumps and ferns. She could have walked it in the dark, their path was so well trodden.

Their walk took them close to the banks of the great Elv River, a sparkling, dancing, fast-moving sea of lights. On sunny holiday days, Grace had taught Budleigh to swim at a point further down river, out of the current, in a large pool of still water close to the bank. He was not scared of the water and skipped along happily, mesmerised by the lights and his mother's gentle voice.

Suddenly, Budleigh's whippet, who had followed them, attempted to fling himself into his arms. In the confusion, Budleigh stepped back and slipped on the muddy bank. Grace lunged forwards to grab the startled child, the puppy nipped at her ankle, maybe in sport or maybe, the dog thought Grace was attacking his beloved master. She swung round and swept the dog from the ground, losing her footing as she did so. Before Budleigh had time to blink, he was on his back on the grass and his mother and pet were in the water. The whippet had caught on a silver birch branch and whimpered pitifully.

Budleigh dived in without a thought for his own safety. He quickly reached the stranded pup, deposited him on the bank and swam swiftly after his mother. Terror made him strong and he quickly reached her. Stretching out his hand, he caught the material of her dress. With all his might, he steered her limp body to the bank. He felt her breath on his neck and was reassured. But just as he stopped to steady his breathing, a biting undercurrent tugged at Grace's heels and almost snatched her from his grip. He thrust out an arm and grabbed her wrist. The dark river gave another tug, followed by another. She opened her eyes and they searched for his. He was there. She relaxed. They looked into each other's eyes for an instant, then her smile of recognition disappeared, as one final tug from the current sucked her silently below the surface, down into the darkness, deep under the water. The river took her from him. She was gone, without a trace, as if she had never been there at all.

Budleigh slowly trod water, while he gazed at the spot where his beloved mother had been. His breath was regular and even, as he held his position in the water. Something so calamitous had just happened, he could not take it all in. "Where had his mother gone? She was there a minute ago," he thought to himself. "I'm sure she was there."

Further time passed. Still she was gone. A heavy weight descended upon him. Slowly, Budleigh began to sink lower and lower into the water, until a great mouthful of river caused him to choke awake. Struggling and scrambling, he made for the bank, but he was so weak and cold, he barely made it out. Halfway out of the water, one arm on the shore, he was dragged by the panting white whippet to the safety of the land.

Several hours later, a very traumatised little boy, carrying a shivering white whippet puppy too tightly, stumbled wetly into his surprised father's arms.

The adult Budleigh watched on, angrily wiping tears from his face with the back of his hand. He could remember the scene as if it were yesterday. He softly and tenderly uttered a single word under his breath: "Mum-a."

Back on the screen, a grim cinema played out. In the matter of a few minutes, a few years passed before him. Budleigh watched on as his father's initial shock and surprise at losing his wife in such a pointless accident, turned to horror, anger and despair. Over time, his grief burrowed into his psyche and took root in a deep-seated anguish and eventually a bitter resentment toward his son that he couldn't conceal. At first, he tried to talk himself out of these feelings with the reasonable side of his mind, "'Ee was only a boy after all," he'd say to himself, over and over again. Some days he'd almost convince himself that he had beaten his own mind. He'd look at the small boy, clinging, terrified to his dog and realise the child shared in the same loneliness, the same grief that cut him like razors. He knew he needed to step up and soothe the desolate boy, be a mum and dad to this child his wife had prayed for for so long, had pined herself almost to death for.

But somehow he couldn't. Every time he looked at the boy, his wounds were cut afresh, raw and smarting as his heart. He lay awake in bed, night after night, churning memories, visions of her, snatching moments of dreams, but always biting awake to the cold reality that was his life. As time went on, the resentment grew like dry rot through his mind. It blackened his thoughts and clouded his judgement, until he couldn't bring himself to look at the child - the child with his mother's eyes, the child whose every action reminded him of her. He fed Budleigh to begin with, but over time, began to leave him to his own devices. Budleigh soon stopped going to school. He spent the days in the woods with his faithful whippet, and the long nights sobbing softly in his attic room. His father's grief made him cruel. He started cuffing the boy as he passed and even took the occasional swipe at his dog, resentful even of this jot of companionship that he himself had been denied.

Fortunately for Budleigh, Mrs James was not to be put off by Salterton Senior's terrifying demeanour and rough bark. She resolutely brought her son Thomas to spend time with Budleigh every weekend. The kind and clever woman noticed Budleigh was losing weight and soon started to take food parcels to the starving boy. These increased in size and started to appear on weekdays too, as the full horror of Budleigh's life became apparent. She understood loss, her own husband having been cruelly taken from her by an evil creeping illness. However, there was no excuse for the way Budleigh was being treated. Mrs James even managed to engineer visits for Budleigh to her house, at first, an afternoon, then a night. Salterton didn't seem to care at first, happy to be rid of this daily reminder of his wife and his wretched life. But just as she thought she may get Budleigh away from his father completely, Salterton senior came hissing to her door, now more animal than human, slavering and raising his hand to her. "Aw ya meddling old trout! Give me back ma boy!!!"

Eventually, Salterton senior beat Mrs James' access to Budleigh back to rare stolen moments, when she'd find the boy alone, but for his thoughts and his dog. He had grown more and more sullen as time went by. His happy smile had turned into a permanent sneer. He barely acknowledged Thomas and Mrs James and had no love in his heart for anything apart from his treasured white whippet, with whom he credited his life.

……….

At sixteen, Budleigh hatched a plan. He'd long since given up worrying what his father thought of him. He wasn't there when he had needed him and now he didn't need him anymore. But he did need a pact, a truce, to ensure that when he walked out of that door for the last time, his father would leave him be, to make the most of whatever tattered strands of life he had left.

It started off well enough.

Late evening sun stretched across the yard, suffusing the wooden table and chairs with a rosy warmth and almost picturesque quaintness. Light picked out particles of dust as they looped and danced in the warm air. Salterton leant on a single slab of pine, sleeves rolled up, putting the final touches to a small carved box he'd been working on for some time. He pressed hard on his little knife, so hard the tips of his fingers whitened, but they still worked quickly, skilfully, Salterton's face screwed up in concentration. At times, he stood slightly, to put more weight behind the cut. The lid was inlaid with a complex pattern of twisted branches and flowers, which seemed to look like faces when he stared at them for too long.

He stopped for a moment, puffed on his intricately carved pipe and swigged from a tumbler of raw grape alcohol he'd brewed himself. He wasn't as drunk as usual and was actually smiling as he looked into the flowers. This fact stuck in Budleigh's mind.

Budleigh, now as tall as a pine sapling struggling for light in the forest's canopy, was not so afraid anymore, He'd fought back a few times, and even won on a couple of occasions. He'd always felt bad about this though, for reasons so complicated that he couldn't even articulate them to himself.

He walked up behind his father. "Hello," he hailed him, so as not to cause surprise. He realised, looking back on this, that he must have harboured just the tiniest slither of hope, even now, that he would be greeted with a note of welcome in his father's eye.

The smile immediately faded from his father's face. It was as if he'd interrupted a private moment Salterton was having. The older man grabbed Budleigh's wrist and twisted it, "What you doin' boy?" Budleigh hated this form of address. 'Boy' was always used with such spite, spat at him: it was no term of endearment, he used the word as a cosh to beat him back down, a reminder of just who was boss. A shiver of pure hatred swept across his fathers face, casting a shadow blacker than death.

All Budleigh thought was that he needed to be free. Free of this grip on his wrist, his life. He groped blindly around with his other hand and felt the rim of something cold. He dabbed at its edge until his fingers closed firmly over the side of a heavy iron pan. He lifted his arm and with a sweeping motion, fuelled by his fathers hatred and the mountain of resentment which now boiled up in him and crystalised in this one movement, he brought the pan down as hard as he could on the back of his father's head.

He felt a momentary surge of triumph, stepped back and stopped, the pan still firmly in his grasp. His father lay still, his eyes open and staring, his head framed with a spreading halo of bright red blood. Budleigh dropped the pan and rushed to help him, but his father was beyond any help the horrified child, or anyone else, could offer. Budleigh's father was dead.

He picked up his dog and ran. He ran and ran and ran and continued running for the rest of his life. Fear and hatred grew inside him until there was nothing left in his heart but a vile bitterness he could no longer control. Budleigh hated the world and almost everything in it. He lived by whatever means he could. Mute for five years, apart from gentle whispering to his only friend, the loving loyal white whippet, the next time he spoke to an actual person he realised he'd acquired a strange stammer. This, however, proved to be the least of his worries.

....

Cord looks from one of his captives to the other and back again. Rexford is, once again, fiddling with the hem of his nightdress, finding it totally absorbing. Budleigh Salterton, the great mean man in black, is crying like a baby. Great torrents of tears whooshing over his tired face, a waterfall of regret and frustration cascading freely for the first time in thirty years.

Cord takes a step back to survey his work. He looks pleased with the broken Budleigh, still sobbing noisily. Of course, Cord can read their minds, so he knows exactly what each of them are thinking, except his certainty in his own skill at reading minds is causing him to miss something very obvious. Something about Rexford should have alerted him to the change in circumstances. While he can indeed read the entirety of Budleigh's mind, there's a tiny bit of Rexford's, that, invisibly, remains out of reach.

Chapter 14

"Time for me to depart," announces Cord. "I'm going to leave you two here for a while, to have a little think. I will return," he adds grandly. With that, Cord is gone, leaving the terrible twosome alone in the thick grey mist.

....

"Think, think - who needs to think? All it ever gets you is into trouble. Thinking is extremely overrated. What do you say, Salterton?" Rexford turned to face Budleigh, who had just about managed to stop crying.

"Salterton. Salterton," hissed Rexford. "I think I've discovered a way to stop Bangle from reading our minds! Salterton!"

Budleigh wasn't listening. He was in a far-off time and place. A place where his mother was gone and his father lay dead before him. Budleigh had buried this memory very, very deeply indeed and its sudden literal reappearance had brought a long suppressed trauma directly to the surface.

"Salterton," insisted Rexford.

Budleigh remained standing stock still, his fists clenched by his side, staring the thousand yard stare. He was attempting, with very limited resources, to process the death of his parents and his part in the tragedy. He was so overwhelmed that he couldn't speak. He could barely

blink, let alone form a coherent sentence, so there he
stood.
Rexford slowly started to walk around the statue of
Budleigh. "Sal-ter-ton," Rexford slowly enunciated. "Sal-
ter-ton," he repeated. He raised a paw and waved it before
Budleigh's eyes. Nothing. Not a flicker.

"Well, well, well. What are we going to do now?" he mused
to himself. "You're about as much use as an umbrella in
a hurricane." Rexford slowly turned around and peered
into the gloom.

Out of the corner of his eye he thought he saw something
move. "What was that?" he muttered to himself, as he
turned his head to where he thought the movement
came from. There, again, just at the periphery of his
vision, a grey blur in the greyness. He turned once more
and started to move toward the blur. He couldn't have
taken more than a few steps, when the gloom started
to disperse, then began to heap up again in amorphous
mounds. "Salterton, Salterton, come over here." Rexford
looked back over his shoulder to where he thought he'd
left Budleigh, only to be greeted with the sight of an
enormous chalky cliff, whose foot he was now standing at.
He turned and ran back the way he thought he'd come,
only to run slap bang into the hard cliff, bending his face
into a serpentine arrangement of planes, totally alien to
a rat.

"Ouch, my snout!" He clasped his nose, cracking it back
into shape and checking for signs of blood. "This isn't
going well," he said to himself, as he pressed his back
against the cliff wall.

From above, a few grains of dirt gently landed on his
head. He reached up a paw and brushed them off. Then a

few more: this time he looked up to see where they were coming from, and just in time, for at that moment, a giant black bird dive-bombed him at high speed, swooping menacingly from the cliff edge above. Running for his life, he only just had time to duck under a nearby bush before he would have been carried away in the bird's giant talons. "That was too close," he thought. "I'm not quite ready to be bird food yet!" He lay back panting, cowering under the meagre branches of a bald black tree. "Budleigh! Budleigh?" he called out hopefully into the air. There was no answer.

Rexford realised, with a gulp, he was on his own. A slight sense of panic welled in his chest: he was actually alone for the first time ever. Rexford hated solitude and did everything he could to ensure it never happened to him. In normal times he had his gang to keep him company, to watch him do things, to be his audience, but now there was just him. "Oh well," he sighed. "Good things come to those who prepare for the the worst." Even he wasn't sure what this meant.

Peering through the wizened branches of the threadbare tree, which at least provided him with some safety, he looked for the bird. After what seemed an age, he said to himself, "I can't stay here all day." His tummy started to rumble. He remembered he hadn't eaten a thing in what felt like days. Garvandulan's kitchen and the ham sandwiches seemed a very long time ago now. "I wish I'd eaten more while I had the chance," he thought, as his stomach gave out a long and ominous growl.

Rexford was so hungry, he decided to make a run for it. About fifty paces away, he could see a small thicket of trees and bushes that would provide him with shelter and maybe even some food. Being a rat, he really wasn't fussy when it came to what he deemed to be food. Even an old shoe would qualify right about now. If he could just get to the trees, he could find some nuts or berries or even an old root to chew on. Looking again for the bird, he could see no sign of it anywhere so, tentatively, he started to move from the relative safety of the bush on to the open ground.

He moved on tiptoes, trying not to make a sound, so that he might not rouse the huge avian predator.

To his credit, Rexford made it about halfway to the copse, before the bird spotted him from its perch, high on the cliff top. Like an expert hang glider, it bounced twice on its claws, gently and gracefully launched itself off the rock face and swooped down toward the sneaking Rexford.

Rex had noticed the bird at just about the same time as it had noticed him, and he immediately took to his heels and ran as fast as his little podgy legs would carry him. He was about twenty paces from the wood, when the bird's sharp talons planted themselves in the dirt before him.

The bird was a huge crow, with glistening jet black feathers and two black beady eyes that stared Rexford to a skidding halt. Rexford managed to stop, just about a beak's length from the giant crow.

"Hello, Rat," said the bird, as it looked Rexford up and down. "Where are you off to in such a hurry? Were you trying to make it into the bushes so I don't eat you?"

"Basically, yes I was," replied Rexford, stunned by his own honesty.

"Where's the fun in that, Rat? Oh that rhymed! CAW

CAW CAW!" cackled the bird, who seemingly liked his own jokes very much. "Do you get it, Rat? Do you? Do you? CAW CAW CAW!"

"Yes I get it. Very good. Ha ha," Rex winced at the sight and sound of the bird guffawing to itself over what was an exceedingly poor 'joke'.

"CAW Caw caw," the bird regained its composure. "Now, what shall I do with you, Rat?"

"Er... be friends with me?" Offered Rexford hopefully.

"Be friends with you! Oh that's very good, CAW CAW CAW!"

The bird was off again, cawing and laughing far harder than Rexford's answer had justified.

"CAW CAW CAW! Be friends with you? CAW CAW CAW!"

Rexford just stood before the bird, waiting for it to stop.

"CAW Caw caw. No, no, Rat. I'm not going to be your friend. I'm going to eat you."

"I thought you might say that," said Rexford, a little dejectedly.

"Yes that's right, Rat, I'm going to eat you. You'll be mainly alive while I pull the flesh from your bones with my sharp beak. Peck-peck-peck I'll go. First your eyes, a lovely hors d'oeuvre, before the main course of your liver. You're nice and fat, so it should be huge. Yum, yum, I'm looking forward to this!"

A small pink tongue shot out from its beak and licked Rexford's face.

"Yuk!" shouted Rexford involuntarily.

"Yum!" rejoined the bird. You are going to make a delicious dinner. A sort of ratatouille! Ratatouille! CAW CAW CAW! Geddit? Ratatouille! CAW CAW CAW."

It was off again, even more pleased with its awful pun than the previous times. Every rat on the planet loathed this stupid , brainless pun. Rexford rolled his eyes, whilst he still could and simply looked at the convulsing corvid.

"CAW CAW CAW! Do you know what, Rat? I haven't had this much fun in ages! CAW CAW CAW! So much fun that I'm going to give you a chance CAW CAW CAW!"

"A chance?" thought Rexford. "A chance is all I need!"

"Answer me this riddle and and I'll spare your life and let you pass. CAW Caw caw."

"Riddle?" thought Rexford. "Riddle? Oh no!" Rexford had never been any good at games or puzzles or riddles. "I'm a gonner!"

"Caw, caw caw. Ok Rat, answer me this:

What's the difference between a princess and a naughty schoolboy? Caw Caw Caw."

The bird took half a step back and looked very pleased with himself, he started to preen in a most self-congratulatory manner, all the while cawing gently to himself.

Rexford, on the other hand, had no such feelings. Although not entirely stupid, he could in no way be described as a thinker. Rexford had got to this disastrous point in his life, with the absolute minimum of thinking. Indeed, if he had stopped to think just a few times, he probably wouldn't be where he was now. Yet here he was, standing before a giant bird being asked to think harder about something than he had ever thought before; he was required to think so hard, that his very life depended on it.

"Why is a princess like a scaughty schoolboy? No, naughty schoolboy! Oh no, I can't even remember the question!" he muttered under his breath.

"What was that Rat? Did you say something? I haven't got all day you know!" The bird peered at him, wings folded, claw tapping impatiently on the ground.

A visibly flustered Rexford searched the corners of his mind for an answer, any answer, any thoughts at all! The corners of his mind were like Budleigh's wash bag, full of crud and seldom used. "Wait a moment, I'm thinking, don't rush me, you're putting me off..."

Rather than applying any serious effort to solving the riddle, Rexford's mind had completely drifted off. Inside his brain, he was skipping through a meadow, gathering berries from bushes, singing happy songs to himself. He really did not do thinking. Snapping to, he realised that he desperately needed a plan B if he was to get out of this. High thinking was something Rex had no capacity for, but low cunning, now, that was a different matter altogether. That he didn't need to think about, it came as naturally as breathing to him.

After a moment or two, he composed himself and stood

before the bird. "Well bird, as you like riddles so much, I have one for you. What is the difference between a bird and a great big stupid idiot?"

The bird cocked his head and looked confused. "No, I'm the one asking the questions, not you."

"You don't know the answer," taunted Rexford. "I can see why being bird brained means being stupid. Stupid like you, you great big stupid bird!"

This was not how it was supposed to be! What always happened, was the bird would find some prey, and it would ask its riddle. The unfortunate animal, would be unable to answer the question and the bird would dismember it on the spot. They were not supposed to answer back and certainly weren't supposed to actively harangue him!

"Come on, come on. I haven't got all day!" Rexford goaded the confused crow. "Come on Mr Stupid. You've ten seconds. Nine. Eight."

"Wait, stop. I need to think," called out the bewildered bird.

"Seven. Six. Five."

"CAW CAW. I can't think under this pressure, Caw!"

"Come on, come on. Think. Think. Before it's too late!"

"CAW! I've got it!"

"Too late, bird!" snarled Rexford, who ran toward the muddled bird and gave it the hardest shove he could manage, kicking it in the leg for good measure, as he barged his way past the tottering avian. With a giant leap, Rexford made the wood and disappeared into the undergrowth.

"Ha ha!" he shouted back behind him. The answer to my riddle is there ISN'T any difference between a bird and a great big stupid idiot! You great big stupid bird!" He laughed and laughed and laughed until his sides ached and he ran out of breath.

The bird sat on his behind, wondering what had just happened. He had been outsmarted by lunch. "I didn't even get the chance to tell him the answer to my riddle. Why is a princess like a naughty school boy?" His ego wounded, he shouted out to Rexford, "The answer to why a princess is like a naughty school boy is that one wears a tiara and the other must try harder!" It was a rotten riddle, but that was the bird for you.

Chapter 15

Rexford was deeply into the trees now, He then remembered he was exceedingly hungry. Casting around for food of any description, he noticed something quite odd to find in a wood. On a branch to the left, appeared to be a picnic basket, made from wicker and draped with a red gingham cloth. Intrigued and extraordinarily hungry, he moved toward the basket and grasped the handle, lifting it from the branch and setting it down on a nearby stump.

"Well, well, well. What have we here? A convenient picnic basket. How fortunate." Rexford looked around for something he could use as a stool' so that he might sit up at the stump and address the basket with his full concentration (though not a thinker, his concentration, when it came to food, was second to none!) Finding a few logs, he fashioned a rough perch and sat down to eat. He was going to enjoy this! He clapped his paws together, and reached for the checked cloth, pulling it from the basket and tucking it into the top of his night dress. He made to open the lid when, from behind him, came a dreadfully familiar voice.

"Hello, Rexford. What are you doing with my lunch?"

Rexford let out a deep sigh, his shoulders slumped. Without turning round he said, "Hello, Cat. I thought you were dead."

Rexford had been asleep the whole time Amelia was

chasing Budleigh around Garvandulan's kitchen, and had missed the whole thing.

"Well, I'm not, Rexford. I'm very much alive and I'm standing behind you!"

The Cat sauntered toward Rex, winding herself in and out of branches and bushes, until she arrived at the stump where Rexford dejectedly sat. "I suppose you're going to eat me now, after batting me round for half an hour first. Soften me up a bit before the coup de grace, a bite to the neck and then it's no more Rex. Gone and completely forgotten."

The Cat sat on her haunches and surveyed the crestfallen rodent. She carefully lifted a grey velvet paw, licking it several times. She wiped it behind her ear and delicately placed it back on the ground. "No Rexford, I'm not going to eat you, I'm going to feed you. Open the picnic basket."

Rexford didn't need telling a second time. With both paws, he flung the lid open and looked inside the basket. What a sight for very sore eyes there was: bread, ham, cheese, pickles, pies, pastries and pate. There were jams and spreads and a large chocolate gateaux to finish. What a feast! At that precise moment, Rexford cared little for whatever motives the Cat may have had in feeding him; he was simply ravenous and he set about the contents of the hamper with gusto.

After a good thirty minutes of chomping and gorging, Rexford began to slow down. He'd managed to get about two thirds of the way through the contents of the hamper, when he realised that he was more than full. So full in fact, that he started to slide off the makeshift stool he'd been sitting on and flopped on to the ground with his legs sticking out in front of him. His eyes started to feel very heavy. Slowly the shutters came down and he drifted off into a deep, deep sleep.

The Cat sat watching. Occasionally she would find some fault in her fur and lick and nibble furiously at an imperceptible imperfection, until she was satisfied that perfection had been restored.

Once Rexford was soundly asleep, the Cat rose, walked over to the snoring rat and sniffed him. She recoiled slightly. Rexford hadn't been near a sink or bath since Garvandulan's and was a bit whiffy. She sniffed again, just to be sure. She didn't actually mind the smell of a ripe rat and would have probably eaten him, had she been hungrier and slightly less principled, but she had bigger fish to fry. She was going to use Rexford as bait.

The thing she really prized was Budleigh Salterton. She had made capturing Budleigh Salterton her number one priority, and she was determined to put her plan into action as soon as she possibly could!

Chapter 16

Budleigh Salterton stood alone, staring into the middle distance for quite a long time. How long, he couldn't be sure, but he knew it had been a while. Slowly, he started to contend with the trauma and events of the last few days. Cord's determination to make him face up to the explosive memories buried deep in his brain, led to Cord clinically excavating them, dragging them out onto the surface and casually blowing them to smithereens.

Budleigh stood among the devastation, surveying the damage to his mind. After a moment, he started to pick at the pieces of shrapnel in his head, carefully collecting each and every shard of memory and sealing them back into the deep, buried place once more. All the little boxes of anxiety that he had stacked, one inside another, were slowly being rebuilt. The wall he carefully constructed around his anger, his frustration and his guilt, the wall it had taken him a lifetime to build, the wall that Cord had surgically destroyed when he made him face all the things he'd neatly stowed away, was going back up.

On one level, Milder would have been proud of the attention to detail Budleigh paid to the construction of this barrier. It was more than a barrier, it was more like a dam. A dam that had been breached by Cord. The flooded plains of his memory were being drained and the dam repaired. Only this time, Budleigh was building it twice as high and twice as thick and twice as wide. No one would ever do that to Budleigh Salterton again!

After a while, he started to regain his composure. His stare went from a thousand yards to a hundred yards, then to a few feet and, finally, he could focus on his immediate surroundings again. He felt his voice return, and his hands relaxed their grip and hung loosely by his side.

With a twist of his head and a crack of his neck, Budleigh took a step forward into the murk and found himself standing at the foot of a very large cliff.

Chapter 17

The events of the recent past had changed Budleigh forever. Far from feeling sorry, he was now burning with the desire for revenge. Cord Bangle had almost broken him. Budleigh cared not one jot which dimension he claimed to be from. Cord had entered his world and nearly destroyed him in the process. If there was one thing Budleigh did better than almost anyone else, it was to harbour a grudge. He elevated hanging on to bad feeling to an art form, and would stop at nothing to get even with the interloper from the fifth dimension!

Budleigh looked around him, he scanned the ground and noticed little ratty footprints in the dusty floor. "Rex-a," he said under his breath. Looking up, he saw, in the near distance, a copse of trees and bushes. Without further pause, he set off for the wood. From above, the large shadow of a giant bird crossed over his own. Before he could look up, the bird had landed and was standing before him.

"Caw caw caw. My, my two in a day! Caw, I'm hoping to have better luck with you. You look a bit tough compared to the other one, but I dare say you'll do. Caw caw caw."

The bird took a step forward. Budleigh held his ground and said, "Listen-a bird. Have you seen a rat in a night dress-a come this-a way?"

"Caw caw caw. What if I have? He called me stupid and

kicked me in the leg Caw caw! I even gave him a chance to live! Ungrateful creature, I should have eaten him on sight. I'm not going to make that mistake again. Now standstill, this won't hurt too much." The mighty bird began to advance on Budleigh.

Budleigh was having none of this and stepped forward to meet the bird head on. With a vicious flick of his ringed right hand, he swung at the bird's head, before it had a chance to peck at his eyes, and knocked it clean out.

"Get-a out of my way-a. I'm-a not in the mood for this-a today!" Stepping over the unconscious crow, Budleigh marched toward the wood.

Chapter 18

After a while, Budleigh found the sleeping Rexford leaning against a tree. His hands were clasped over his belly and he was snoring loudly.

"Rex-a, Rex-a! Wake up-a!" Budleigh grasped Rex by the ears and gave him a shake. Rexford spluttered into consciousness and blearily came to.

"Ah, Salterton, what kept you? Do you want some food? I think there's some left." Rexford waved an arm in the general direction of where the picnic basket had been. But it was gone.

"No-a, I don't-a want any food-a. Listen to me Rex-a, I've had enough of this place-a. We're-a getting out of here-a now-a! What were-a you telling me about blocking-a Bangle from our thoughts-a? How did you-a do it?" Budleigh's tone was very insistent and Rexford could see he was serious and very angry.

"Well old chap, I discovered, quite by chance, that if, in my mind, I hide my thoughts in plain sight, Bangle would overlook them. He has the arrogance of a man who thinks he knows it all. He thinks we're easy to read, because to him, we are, but this has also made him lazy and a little careless."

Budleigh was struggling to understand what he meant. Rexford could see the look of puzzlement in his eyes. "Ok, let me explain. A while back, when we were falling once again, I had some quite terrible thoughts about Bangle. Thoughts so awful, there was no way he could have ignored them, especially as he's so flipping self-righteous. But for some reason, he didn't notice them. This seemed very strange to me as, at the time, he was busily picking holes in both of us, poking around in the back of our minds, yet my thoughts remained opaque to him. I then had this sudden flash of inspiration. It really took me back, because I rarely have flashes of anything, let alone inspiration!"

Budleigh was looking at Rex with a 'get on with it' face. Rex took the hint.

"Well, I revisited the thoughts I'd had about Bangle, to see what made them so different from all the other bad feelings I harbour about him. Do you know what the difference was this time? This time, rather than imagine the worst thing I could think about Bangle, in my mind, I made him look ridiculous. Like a gone-wrong clown, a rag doll to be tossed around, a great stupid moron, a figure of fun. In my mind, I made him ridiculous and he didn't notice. Maybe he couldn't possibly believe that anyone could see him that way, and I'm not surprised. His ego is so massive, I dare say being laughed at is something he simply couldn't imagine."

Budleigh poked a finger at the brim of his top hat and pushed it upwards, while he let this information sink in.

"So, are you-a saying that if-a we make him look-a ridiculous in our minds, he can't-a read our thoughts-a?"

"That's precisely what I'm saying. His ego won't let him look stupid, even if it's there right in front of him!"

"Well-a, this-a changes everything-a!" Budleigh yanked
down the brim of his hat over his brow and stood tall.

"Rex-a. We're getting-a out of here-a and we're taking-a
Bangle with us-a!

Chapter 19

The Cat had been sitting, statue-still, behind a tall pine. She could see Budleigh and Rexford in deep conversation. Her plan had worked and Budleigh Salterton, her own murderer, was now within striking distance. She crept back behind the tree and waited.

Amelia knew she would have to be careful. She knew if she wasn't, the hunter might become the hunted. She hadn't really expected to see them so animated. As she recalled they weren't really friends; hadn't Budleigh tried to shoot Rexford too? But sometimes, my enemy's enemy is my friend and so it seemed on this occasion. 'Never mind,' she thought, a Boggis was more than a match for a couple of scruffs like these two.

Following his experience at the hands of Cord, something had changed in Budleigh; something profound had happened inside his brain. Never a stupid man, Budleigh had always felt held back by his awful start in life. School was a fleeting memory. He has spent far more time as an itinerant ne'er-do-well than he had being educated and this deficiency had defined his whole adulthood.

The odd thing was that Cord's horror show hadn't had the effect Cord had desired on Budleigh. Instead of softening him, it had actually hardened his view of himself and the world around him. If anything, being shown his own life left him feeling vindicated, justified and just plain right about the decisions he took and the way he lived his life.

This all gave Budleigh a new-found sense of clarity of thought and action.

The Cat slunk around the edge of the clearing. Rexford was lying on his back, in the same spot he'd gorged on her picnic. His legs were in the air and his eyes, shut. Budleigh was nowhere to be seen.

Her hackles rose, as she crept closer to the supine rat. She knew it was a trap, but she also knew she was a Boggis and could not be overcome by a rodent and an old man.

Moving stealthily on her belly, she cleared the ground between them in seconds. When she was within pouncing distance, she leapt nimbly, bared her teeth, and picked up Rexford softly in her mouth.

"GERK!" cried Rexford. His day had just gone from bad to worse!

He'll be useful as a hostage," she said out loud, even though her mouth was full. Cats' manners are often appalling.

At that moment, Budleigh sprang from behind a bush, catching the Cat with a blow to the back of the head so hard, she instantly fell to the ground, spitting out Rexford in shock. Rexford shot across the picnic site and narrowly avoided being crushed by her giant falling frame as she landed in a heap on a pile of pine needles.

Budleigh strode over to the crumpled cat, grabbed her by the scruff of the neck and wrenched her from her needley nest.
"Overstreet, get-a the bag."

Rexford lay on the floor gasping for breath, his screwed up nightdress around his neck. He struggled up on to one elbow.

"Rexford. The bag-a!"

Rexford had no idea what he was talking about. "What are you playing at Salterton? I was nearly eaten!"

"BAG," insisted Salteron, who shot out an arm and pointed at his large brown Gladstone bag, which had mysteriously appeared in the clearing beside them.

"How did that get there?!" exclaimed Rexford.

"Open it and bring it here," ordered Budleigh.

Rexford staggered to his feet and made his way over to the bag. He tried to lift it and was surprised at just how heavy it was. Struggling, he dragged it over to where Budleigh held the limp Amelia.

Budleigh drew the Cat level with his own face. She was still unconscious, which made her so much easier to handle. "She'll-a be planning to escape-a, as soon as she comes to-a," he said.
"Quickly, let's-a get out of here-a and go back into the gloom. She can't escape from that-a!"

"Salterton, what are you going to do to it?" shouted Rexford.

"Why-a I'm-a going fishing-a. And when-a you fish-a, you need a little bait-a!"
Budleigh picked up the bag and headed out of the wood, past where the crow had fallen and walked very

deliberately into the middle of the gloom.

Rexford raced to keep up with him, "Wait, Salterton. I've only got little legs!"

Budleigh looked around. "Yes-a. Here-a," he grunted, dropping the bag to the ground. He locked his hands together, stretched his arms against them and cracked his knuckles, loudly. Relaxing his grip, he unlocked his hands and folded his arms.

"Now what?" said Rexford.

"Now-a? Now we-a wait."

Chapter 20

Neither Budleigh nor Rexford really had any idea where they were: not in time or space or dimension. So much had happened since the beginning of the incarceration and exile, they were totally disorientated. It seemed fitting they now found themselves standing in the gloom.

The gloom couldn't really be described as a landscape - it was very far from that. It wasn't really a place at all, as far as their understanding of what constituted a 'place'. There was no visible sun or point of illumination. Light was diffuse and left no discernible shadows. There were no clouds in the sky, only a greyness that seemed to have no edge. There was no horizon, or any sort of feature that you could make out at all. Sound was muffled and indistinct. The words they occasionally uttered to each other fell, leaden, into the grey dusty surface of the land around them. If you were even a few feet away, you could not be heard. A few feet further and you would be lost in the great glower.

The gloom was an uncomfortable place to be. Mixed in among the greyness, was a sense of a great discomfort, a foreboding that seemed just out of reach.

"I've got a bad feeling about this place Budleigh. Can't we do this somewhere else? I'm freezing too. What's left of this nightshirt isn't offering me much warmth in all this damp murk." Rexford wrapped his arms around himself in a vain effort to keep warm. He started to shiver.

"No-a," replied Budleigh. "It has to be here-a." Budleigh sniffed the air in anticipation.

He was truly changed from the man he once was. Before, he was largely itinerant. He had wandered about the land, going after what easy pickings he could scavenge: an old lady's purse here, a child's birthday money there. His life was totally aimless; he had no ambition or thought for tomorrow. He lived purely in the now.

Some might think that living entirely in the present was something to be envied, a state that some strive their whole lives to emulate. But what those people overlook is that to really live constantly in the moment, denies you the opportunity to either plan ahead or, more importantly, to draw lessons from your past. The consequence of living like this was you never progress, you remain fixed in a stasis. Frozen at the point when you abandoned the future and disregarded the past. Budleigh had become stuck.

He had not realised how stuck he was until the moment that Cord had made him face his past. That seemed to unlock something in him that had lain dormant for many many years. The feeling he'd buried for so long stirred in him. There soon followed a tidal wave of emotion, which very nearly overwhelmed him and washed him away...

His reaction had been predictable and very 'Budleigh Salterton'. He'd immediately started to repack all the thoughts and emotions he'd buried away. He built the walls higher, wider, and thicker than before, with one solitary exception.

Budleigh had made a conscious decision not to pack away something that was driving him on to try to capture Cord

Bangle, the most powerful being in his universe.

When Budleigh was wandering the land, living for the moment, he had no real sense of the passage of time. One day rolled into the next and the next and the next. This made his life banal and trivial. No matter what he may have thought about the recent events that had led him to this particular point in his life, you could in no way describe them as banal. For the first time in a long time, longer than he could remember, he actually felt *something*. For what seemed like the longest moment, he'd felt nothing, just endless ennui and boredom, but now, here, he felt alive. Surely this should have led him to want to thank Cord Bangle, to shake him by the hand, to warmly embrace him as a brother, to profusely apologise for all the hurt he'd caused. Cord had said as much when they last spoke, but none of this had happened, because the demon Budleigh failed to pack away with the other bits of his personality he couldn't stand, was fear.

Fear of the other, fear of power, fear of being found out and fear of Cord Bangle. Budleigh Salterton was terrified of Cord Bangle. The great whiteness that always heralded Cord's arrival only served to highlight the darkness that followed his departure. A darkness that, at times, enveloped him. When it did, that's when he was at his most dangerous. And right now, Budleigh was surrounded by a pitch blackness like he had never known before.

Chapter 21

They waited ….. and they waited …..and they waited. In fact, they waited so long, they redefined the word 'waited', remodelled it until it meant something more like 'were tortured'. Finally, there was a stirring in the gloom. Not much at first, just a tiny ripple in the distance. Rexford was the first to notice.

"Budleigh, what's that?" Rex shot out an arm in the direction of the ripple. "There, again. Do you see it?"

Budleigh peered hard in the direction Rex was pointing. He screwed his eyes up and concentrated on the small patch of grey. Then, out of the corner of one eye, Budleigh did see something. A darting small shape, he couldn't make out the form of the object as it was too indistinct and far off.

"There again, Salterton, another!" Rexford was spotting more and more of the shapes. They distorted the gloom as they moved through it. It was as if they were behind a curtain and you could see them running alongside it. Now, even Budleigh could see them. They were everywhere, darting around them like fireworks going off underwater. First this way, then that. They were starting to make a noise too now. It was actually less of a noise and more of low moan, doppler shifted, so that they sounded like morbid ambulances careening through the gloom.

"What's going on, Budleigh? I really don't like this!" A

very rattled rat ran behind Budleigh Salterton and hid behind his legs, clutching at the material of his trousers.

"It's-a beginning Rex-a. It's starting-a."

Rexford didn't like the sound of this, but there was very little he could do, so he clung a little tighter to Budleigh and waited to see what was going to happen.

Objects in the distance spun closer and closer - or did they? It was difficult to tell just how far away they were. The gloom precluded any idea of scale or depth. The seeping dank half-light had no horizon, giving few clues. It was almost impossible to judge sizes. Sometimes the objects felt very far away, sometimes they seemed startlingly close. Still they continued. Around and around they went.

"I'm starting to feel a little dizzy," Rexford croaked. He had gone a very odd colour and was looking bilious. "Just-a hold on to my leg-a Rex-a."

Without warning, the shapes started to slow. One by one they wound down to a stand still. They began to form a group. Other larger shapes joined them, starting to form ranks, five or six deep and maybe thirty or forty wide. Together, they advanced on Budleigh and Rexford. Slowly but surely they slid toward them. The noise they initially made resembled the sea at low tide, gently undulating waves washing in, one after another on a soft sandy beach, every seventh wave, slightly louder than the preceding six. In this rhythm they advanced, one step forward, half a step back and on the seventh, a full step forward and no step back.

As they advanced, Budleigh and Rexford began to be able to make out the outlines of faces. Yes, faces: beautiful, ugly, old, young, women, children, men. The ranks of faces, stacked one on top of another, continued to advance in waves toward them. Somewhat soothing noises, gave way to a more insistent washing back and forth. It grew louder and louder; individual voices clanging through the chorus. It was not possible to make out what they were saying, as there were too many other voices, all talking over the top of each other.

"Let's get out of here, Budleigh, I really don't like this!" shouted Rexford, against the ever growing howl.

"Stand-a your ground!" Budleigh bawled back.

The faces' advance continued. They grew closer and larger and higher, until, before them there stood a vast wall of baying mouths, fathomless faces, cavernous eyes all firmly fixed on Budleigh Salterton. A great gale came from their noise, making it increasingly difficult for either to stand up. Indeed, Rexford was just starting to lift from the ground, his legs trailing behind him, arms clutching crazily about Budleigh's leg, when Budleigh raised his arms and, like a conductor, with a slicing motion brought the noise to an abrupt halt.

Rexford immediately hit the ground, face first, as the wind instantly stilled.

For a moment, there was silence, while both sides caught their breath.

Budleigh broke the silence, "Who are-a you-a?" he shouted up at the vast wall of faces.

"We," said the wall, "are the people of The Wall." So immense was The Wall, that even though the faces spoke

in unison, it took a long time for the words to reach
Budleigh and Rexford's ears, giving an effect not unlike
a large wave breaking over a very long beach. You could
hear the answer coming towards you and receding into
the distance.

"How-a did you come to be-a here-a?"

Somewhere in the distance you could hear a great
laughter coming.

"Rex-a cover your ears-a!" shouted Budleigh, clapping his
own hands over his ears.

"Why?" started Rexford, before a literal gale of laughter
hit them. Budleigh just about remained on his feet, but
Rexford, taken a little off guard, ended up rolling off, over
and over in the dirt. He managed to get his paws over
his ears, just as the peal of laughter passed them and
headed off into distance. Picking himself up and dusting
himself off, he stumbled back to Budleigh's side. Shaking
his head, his ears still ringing from the laughter, Rexford
shouted up at the Wall "Do you mind not doing that?" The
Wall glanced at Rex, but took no further notice of him.
"Charming!" thought Rexford to himself.

"How?" said The Wall. "How did you come to be here?"

This sent a ball of fear rolling across Budleigh's chest,
down his legs and into his toes. "What do they mean, old
chap?" Rexford enquired.

""How long-a have you been-a here?" Budleigh tried
again.

"We have always been here," The Wall shivered. "There's

a spot reserved for those who are lost." Their ranks part and a Budleigh Salterton shaped hole appears in The Wall."

"Hey hang on... What about me?" Rexford sounded genuinely wounded.

"Rex-a you idiot, don't-a you realise what this is-a?"

"A big wall of shouty faces that I'm not allowed to join?"

"Rex-a you fool, this isn't a holiday camp-a. It's a monumental trap-a! It's-a limbo, a place of no escape-a, you'll be part of this wall-a for ever-a! Cursed to spend your days-a as part-a of this vast-a hive of faces. You-a won't be you anymore-a, you'll permanently be just another-a face in the crowd-a!"

"I won't," replied Rexford. "They don't want me. It's you they're after..." Rexford peered around him at the huge hands making their way toward Budleigh. Salterton spun round just in time to see the massive hands about to close in on him.

"Oh-a no-a you don't-a!" Budleigh grabbed for his bag, opened it, reached inside, pulled out a blinking Amelia and thrust her at the Wall. "Here-a, take this-a!"

The Wall instantly recoiled in collective fear at the sight of Amelia.

"Where did you get that?" The edges of The Wall were starting to recede "You shouldn't have that. You'll make him come here. Put it away!"

Budleigh advanced a few paces, thrusting the exhausted

cat in front of him. "What's-a the matter? Frightened of this-a bedraggled kitty-a?"

The Wall was now in full flight. As quickly as it had arrived it was gone, leaving Budleigh, Rexford and Amelia standing alone in the gloom.

Alone, that is, until a great whiteness began to descend upon them. It seems The Wall was right: he *was* coming!

Chapter 22

All they can see is white. No up or down or this way or that, just white. Everything is white. It's an odd whiteness. Not so bright as to dazzle, but bright enough so that there are no features, no shadows or textures, only white. A murmuring, breathy white.

"Oh no... What have you done!" exclaims Rexford. "I'm not sure how much more I can take!"

"Remember, what-a you told me Rex-a? Remember? Now-a, now is the time to think-a those thoughts. Think-a them now-a Rex!"

Rexford crouches down, screws his eyes tightly shut and thinks the most ridiculous things about Cord he can.

Meanwhile, Budleigh thinks his own thoughts and readies himself for the imminent arrival.

Cord Bangle appears right on cue. First an arm, then a shoulder, followed by a leg, torso and finally a head.

"You two again! Oh dear, what *am* I to do with you?" Cord seems more than a little weary. Has he to continue to keep both of them locked up even longer? It seems they'd learned nothing while they'd been in his care.

"Budleigh, put Amelia down. Gently!"
Budleigh looks at Amelia, who is still in his grasp. She

is exhausted and limp. He then turns to look at Cord. "You-a want this-a?" He shakes Amelia in Cord's general direction.

"Put her down Salterton," Cord insists. Usually he has a smile not too far from his lips, but today, it is gone. "Put. Her. Down."

"This-a? You want-a me to put-a this down-a? Ok, here-a you go." He chucks the limp cat at Bangle. She lands in a heap at his feet. Cord immediately bends down and picks her up. "Amelia, Amelia, are you all right? Amelia opens an eye and looks at Cord.

"I'll be ok. Worry about Salterton. He's not the same man he once was. He's dangerous and he's after you." She closes her eyes and falls into unconsciousness.

"Fear not, old friend, I'm ready for him." Cord gently lies Amelia down beside him.

"Are-a you, Bangle? Are you-a?"

"Do you think I'm scared of you, Salterton? I'm from a different dimension! To me you are flatter than a playing card. I can see right through you! There's nothing you can do to me!"

"Is that-a so?"

Cord looks at Rexford, crouching as if he is getting ready for take off.

He scans Rexford's mind and sees that there is nothing going on in there. Unsurprised, he turns to Budleigh and says very determinedly, "Yes, that is so."

Chapter 23

Before Cord's arrival, Budleigh had been thinking about the inter dimensional being and his method of entering and leaving this world. How did he manage to hop from one dimension to another with such apparent ease? Was he some kind of magician, able to wave a wand and make himself appear and disappear at will? Budleigh had never heard him utter "Abracadabra!" or any such incantation. He'd never even seen anything that even vaguely resembled a wand.

So, how did he do it? Thinking back to all the times they'd encountered Cord, Budleigh began to piece bits together. He started with the thing he knew most about, Cord's exits from scenes. They were as dramatic as his entrances. On the occasions he and Rexford had followed Cord out into wherever it was he went to, he couldn't actually remember too much about the process. He could remember being in the room and he could remember falling, but the bit in the middle was very sketchy. Was it a door they went through? Well it sort of was, only he didn't remember it having any edges or handles or frame. It was more like a tent flap, a curtain that could be parted. Except that on some occasions it *was* like a door, a sliding door. But which was it? Budleigh thought harder.

When the whiteness descended, it took a while for Cord to appear. Sometimes, it would be as if he'd put his head through a curtain. At other times, it would seem as if he were stepping out of a shower, first one leg then his body and then his head. Budleigh thought hard about doors and curtains and keys and locks. He didn't understand how Cord moved about, apparently appearing out of thin air, but he did know that everything changed when Cord was near.

Chapter 24

Budleigh is now watching Cord very intently.

"Well Salterton, I can see that you have learned absolutely nothing from my efforts to help you. I see we're going to have to extend your time with us. We can't have you rampaging around Rattopia, now can we?"

"Oh-a, why not-a? I ask-a again, who are you-a to tell me what-a to do-a? On whose authority do you act-a?"

"Authority? My own of course! I'm from a higher plane! It is my duty to help you!" Cord smiles beneficently at Budleigh.

Budleigh rolls his eyes. "Duty-a? Duty! Duty to imprison-a and torture me? No-a trial or jury has-a convicted me-a of anything-a. It's purely at your whim-a that you keep me-a hostage here-a! What of your-a people? What do-a they think-a about your-a behaviour? Who judges the judge?"

"My people?" Cord looks slightly taken aback. He wasn't expecting to have a discussion about morals with possibly the most amoral man he'd ever met!

Instinctively, Budleigh senses a chink in Cord's persona, and he goes all out to turn that chink into the largest crack he can manage. Cord's own tactics, in attempting to get Budleigh to face up to his behaviour, are now being used on him!

"Yes-a, your people? What do they think-a about you-a marauding about the place-a, interfering in other people's lives-a? Is this a normal thing-a where you're from-a? And where exactly ARE-a you from-a?"

Cord drops his head slightly and takes a breath. Lifting his eyes, he looks at Budleigh. He stares at him for a moment. Has he underestimated this being? He tries to scan Budleigh's mind, only something is not quite right. He tries again. Nothing. Budleigh is using the technique Rexford had unwittingly stumbled upon. He is, at this moment, imagining Cord, the masterful inter-dimensional space Lord, naked and being tickled by the twelve footmens' twelve feather dusters.

"What are you doing Salterton?" an increasingly anxious Bangle asks.

"Don't you know-a?" Budleigh raises an eyebrow and takes half a step forward.

"Y-yes, yes of course I do." Cord sounds less convinced this time.

"Answer my-a question then-a," persists Budleigh, taking another step to the left.

"Where do I come from? I'm not sure I can explain in a way that you would understand. My world is on a higher-dimensional plane. The things you see and touch here are as shadows in my realm. A colourful cartoon we peer into. It's like watching a screen: all the elements are recognisable but they remain behind glass and we cannot touch or influence the events. We are passive viewers of

your world. We see the mistakes you make, the harm you cause to each other, and yet we are powerless to prevent it."

"Although we are from a higher plane, we are not so different from you, except in one respect. Many millennia ago, we were as you are now. We fought each other in great battles. Many of us died needless, futile deaths over nothing of any consequence. We fought and fought until there were but a few hundred of us left."

"We could war no more and we decided, as a people, that we would end this pointless slaughter and seek to forge a peace that would be lasting, just and bring fairness and equality to all of our citizens. It wasn't easy to achieve. Many millions had died. Opinion and feelings ran very deeply. It took over a hundred of your years to finally agree a settlement that was binding and permanent. Never again did we wage war on ourselves, or anyone else. We've lived in peace and harmony ever since and over time, we started to evolve in ways no one could have expected, until we outgrew the need for our physical bodies and moved into the higher dimension we inhabit today."

All the while Cord is telling his story, Budleigh Salterton is gradually making his way between Bangle and the place he had emerged from.

"So-a where are the rest of you-a?"

"The rest of us? Why there are no 'the rest of us.' We are all here now! When we stopped needing our bodies to live, we found that we had all come to inhabit the same space. I am still Cord Bangle, but I am also everybody else that

exists on this plane, so, there isn't anyone else as such, only we."

"Then-a how do you have-a a body and a head-a?" Salterton is now squarely between Bangle and the exit.

"That is for your benefit, for without a physical form you might not know that we are even here!"

"That-a suits me just fine-a!" With that, Budleigh kicks the door slam shut! For the first time, Bangle actually looks worried "What are you doing?"

"Don't-a you know-a, space man-a?"

Cord reaches into his pocket and begins to fiddle with something. Seeing his chance, Budleigh calls to Rexford. "Now-a, Rex! Now!"

Rexford springs up from his crouching place and grabs Cord around the neck. Cord is thrown off balance and begins to teeter about in the greyness. Budleigh strides forward and grabs Bangle's arm.

"What-a have we here-a?!" Salterton thrusts his hand into Cord's pocket and pulls out a small metal lock. In the lock hole is a kitten with a curled tail.

"Don't touch that!" pleads Bangle. Rexford is still hanging round his neck and Budleigh is holding the rather puny being easily at arm's length.

"Why ever not-a? Is it important-a?"

"Yes it's very important - without it I can't..." Cord's voice trails off, as he realises that he has given far too much away.

"Go on-a, space-a man. What-a can't you do-a? Is it go

home-a? Can't you go home-a?!" A cruel grin comes to Budleigh's thin lips, which he licks with relish at the thought that he has captured the mighty Cord Bangle!

Bangle looks horrified. If Salterton pulls the key-ty from the lock, he will indeed be unable to return to the fifth dimension and there will be worse to come!

"Now Salterton, you don't know what you're doing…"

"Ah, here-a we go again-a. You-a telling me-a I don't know what I'm doing-a. Well-a let me tell you-a spaceman, that I know exactly what-a I'm doing-a! I'm going to take-a you hostage-a and we're going to get out of here-a and go home-a. And then-a, without your infernal meddling-a I, Budleigh Salterton, will exact a terrible revenge-a on that girl-a and all that-a she stands for-a. Your people may-a have stopped fighting-a, but I haven't! He throws back his head and gives a chilling laugh.

"Don't forget me!" shouts Rexford, who has let go of Bangle now and is standing beside Budleigh. "I've got a few scores to settle too. There's a pompous preening prat who's long overdue his comeuppance!"

"So-a space-a man. What happens if-a I pull-a this key-a out of this lock-a?"

"Don't" cries Bangle. "Please don't!"

Budleigh lightly grabs the chain dangling from the kitten's curled tail.

"What-a, you mean this-a?"

"Don't!"

Budleigh stares Bangle in the eye and gives the chain the gentlest of tugs.

"Whoops-a!"

The key pops from the lock and dangles from the end of Budleigh's outstretched finger.

A microsecond later, the whiteness evaporates: Budleigh, Rexford, Cord and Amelia fall, slowly at first, then faster and faster through the void, until, in the distance, Rexford sees the outline of a familiar place. A dim amber light slowly flashes in the distance and a green radar screen scans endlessly in the half-light. Rexford's office is coming toward them at an alarming speed!

Closer and closer they scream towards the room, faster and faster, Rexford closes his eyes and braces for impact. Budleigh Salterton's eyes are wide open, his hands clenched in fists by his side, his thoughts clear.

He is ready for this!